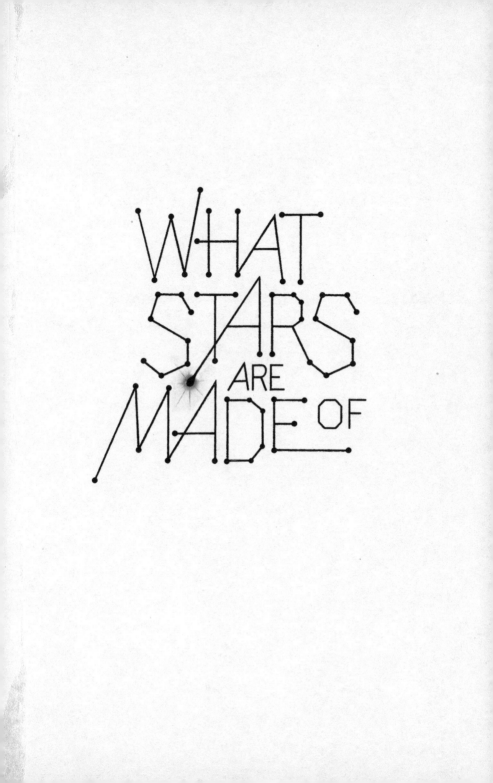

WHAT STARS ARE MADE OF

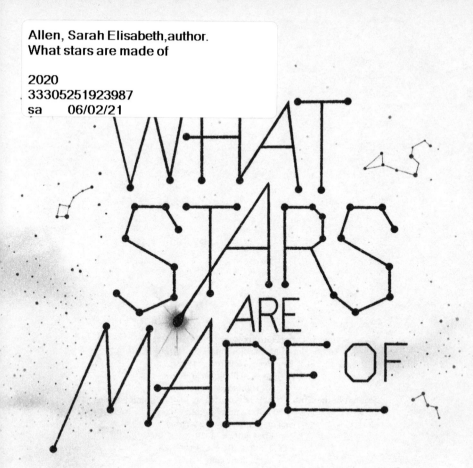

WHAT STARS ARE MADE OF

Sarah Allen

Farrar Straus Giroux

New York

Farrar Straus Giroux Books for Young Readers
An imprint of Macmillan Publishing Group, LLC
120 Broadway, New York, NY 10271
Copyright © 2020 by Sarah Allen
Printed in the United States of America by LSC Communications,
Harrisonburg, Virginia
Designed by Monique Sterling
First edition, 2020
1 3 5 7 9 10 8 6 4 2
mackids.com
Library of Congress Cataloging-in-Publication Data

Names: Allen, Sarah Elisabeth, author.
Title: What stars are made of / Sarah Allen.
Description: First edition. | New York : Farrar, Straus and Giroux, 2020. |
Summary: Twelve-year-old Libby, born with Turner syndrome, is determined
to win a science contest and use the money to help her older sister's
growing family, while surviving middle school.
Identifiers: LCCN 2019013249 | ISBN 9780374313197 (hardcover)
Subjects: | CYAC: Middle schools—Fiction. | Schools—Fiction. |
Sisters—Fiction. | Turner syndrome—Fiction. | Genetic
disorders—Fiction.
Classification: LCC PZ7.1.A4394 Wh 2020 | DDC [Fic]—dc23
LC record available at https://lccn.loc.gov/2019013249

Our books may be purchased in bulk for promotional, educational, or
business use. Please contact your local bookseller or the Macmillan Corporate
and Premium Sales Department at (800) 221-7945 ext. 5442 or by email at
MacmillanSpecialMarkets@macmillan.com.

To Martine, who saw the story I really
wanted to write and showed me how.

And to all the girls like Libby.
I wrote this for you.

An Anti-Grinch Gets Excited

I was born with a heart three sizes too big.

No, really. Like an Anti-Grinch. Like it was already shouting, *I'M JUST TRYING REALLY HARD OVER HERE*.

Mom tells me she was very, very scared for her baby girl. But twelve years later, I'm still here.

There were a whole buttload of other weird things happening to me when I was born, too. But it's not like that's what I go around thinking about all the time, especially on a day when my mom and dad tell me they have a surprise unbirthday present waiting for me after school.

This is what happened when I woke up this morning:

Mom made chocolate Malt-O-Meal for breakfast. That is my all-time favorite food.

Dad looked up from his book and grinned at me—a mysterious grin like he was hiding a secret.

Then Mom put a bowl of the delicious, steamy Malt-O-Meal in front of me and said, "Guess what, Libby."

I was already on my third bite so I had to swallow before I could say, "What?"

"We're not going to tell you what it is, but there is going to be a surprise waiting for you when you get home from school today."

I put down my spoon. "You're buying me a puppy, aren't you?"

Dad laughed, looking back at his book. "Honestly, I think you'll like it as much as that."

So it was something good. Really good. Maybe a safari in Botswana? Maybe it had something to do with my big sister, Nonny, who lived in Chicago with her husband, Thomas. Maybe it was a pet iguana? A pet iguana would be one of the most unique pets ever. I would name her Rosalind after Rosalind Franklin. She's a scientist too many people don't know about. When I come across important, special, underestimated people like Rosalind, I collect them in my head and they become my friends. Then I have a whole squad of friends going around with me wherever I go. I talk to them a lot. I ask them questions, I tell them what I'm worrying about, and I try to figure out what the best of them would do.

So Rosalind the Iguana would only be one of many awesome names I could choose from.

I rubbed my hands together. "I have lots of good guesses," I said.

"Yeah?" said Mom. "Like what?"

I tried to do the same mysterious grin that my dad did, and then shoved another bite of Malt-O-Meal in my mouth. Dad laughed again. Mom did a small hop as she walked back over to the sink. I bounced in my seat a couple of times, feeling almost like it really was my birthday.

I like watching my mom in the kitchen. It's like watching those YouTube videos of Michelle Kwan ice-skating in the Olympics. Mom has broad shoulders and round, strong arms and sometimes she says she feels "stocky" or "ungraceful," but she's not like that in the kitchen. In the kitchen she's a ballerina.

Mom also has:

1. Short, curly hair that's graying on the sides.
2. A wide smile.

3. Her own bakery that she started when I was four years old. She told me she'd wanted to start one for a long time, but she was scared. She didn't really know how to do the business stuff. When I was four, Dad told her she should just do it. Totally go for it. So she did.

Dad is an art teacher at the high school. Once I'm in ninth grade I could maybe take a class from him, except I'm probably the worst person at art in the whole school. I'm not so great with *fine motor skills*. That's okay, though. I'm better at using microscopes and not being one bit afraid that time we dissected cow eyeballs.

Dad also has:

1. A bald pate (*pate*, one of our Hard Reading Words from English that's basically a fancy word for the top of someone's head).
2. Round glasses.
3. At least twenty books about Vincent van Gogh.
4. A voice that is quiet but never, ever shaky.

My parents are pretty smart.
And good at knowing the best surprises.

My Best Friend Is a Room

On most days, I am a Front-Row-Sitter, a Note-Taker, a Volunteer-Whiteboard-Writer, an Answer-Knower. On most days I never have to be told to stay still, at least not more than once. Except on days when my mom and dad tell me that there is a surprise waiting for me. Then sitting still is like trying to wash a cat.

Except in Ms. Trepky's class.

Everyone sits still in Ms. Trepky's class. It's only the third week of school, but we all know that.

Ms. Trepky is tall. Taller than Mom and Dad by at least half a foot. And she is skinny. She has a long nose and long fingers and near-black hair cropped short in a very clean bob. Her face is smooth and pale white like porcelain, and she has a way of looking at you like she's really seeing you, like she knows what you're thinking and what's really going on inside. So I stayed in my seat, even on After-School Surprise Day.

So it's not a puppy? Maybe a kitten? Maybe it's a vacation? A trip to NASA headquarters! A trip to Antarctica to see seals and penguins and—

"Libby!"

I jumped, and a couple of kids behind me giggled.

Ms. Trepky was standing right in front of me.

"I'm sorry, Ms. Trepky," I said. "Could you please repeat the question?" I'd managed to stay in my seat, but the Attentive-Listener part of myself wasn't doing so great.

"Who said, 'You must do the thing you think you cannot do'?"

The Answer-Knower wasn't her normal self, either. I had to say three words I don't like to say. I looked down and folded my hands. "I don't know."

Ms. Trepky looked at me for a few seconds, then stepped to the front of the classroom, right in front of the world map.

In Ms. Trepky's class we do American history. History is a medium subject for me—not the best, but not the worst. I like that it's about remembering and memorizing things. I'm good at remembering things like dates and presidents' names and every muscle in your leg. So that part is good, but it's not like in science, where it's remembering *and* discovering weird and surprising new things that might one day help the world. I'm not really sure what people can *do* with history.

But at least it's interesting most of the time. At least it means that there are new people to talk to in my head. Like that time at the beginning of last school year when my class went on a hike in Boulder Canyon. Even though most people in Colorado like hiking a lot, it's not something I'm super-awesomely great at, because if I go *too* hard my heart starts pounding and my lungs feel like they're in a steel cage. Basically, on that hike a lot of the other kids were going faster and faster, so I stayed toward the back where some of the slow adults could see me, and I talked to my friend Sacagawea. In case you didn't know, Sacagawea was an awesome woman from the Shoshone tribe who helped some Virginian explorers who didn't know where to go. Sacagawea is a very supportive hiking buddy.

So in Ms. Trepky's class, I get even more new people to think about and imagine and talk to.

People to hike with or to help me when I have questions. And at least it's not math.

Maybe it's strange that I like science and not math, because a lot of people think they go together. And maybe they do, but when I see a math worksheet my brain refuses to budge. Sometimes it happens with writing assignments, too, unless the teacher has made it very clear what we're supposed to write about, like Ms. Trepky does. With science, though, it's not about guessing what the teacher wants, trying to figure out their sneaky expectations or what they *wish* you'd written about. In science, you simply follow the instructions and do the experiments. In science, you try again. In science, you have fun.

At the front of the room, Ms. Trepky folded her long, elegant fingers together.

"It's time to start discussing your semester projects," she said.

Groans from the back row. Dustin Pierce, the loudest groaner, said, "But it's the beginning of the school year."

Ms. Trepky stood still until the groans stopped. "I am aware of that fact, Mr. Pierce," she said. "However, these are not last-minute throw-together projects. You will have to work on these consistently throughout the first half of the year if you're going to get the grade you want."

More groans. Ms. Trepky folded her long fingers together again and the scuffling and whispering stopped quickly.

"For your semester projects, you will each select a figure from our textbook. A person you find more than merely interesting. This will be someone you relate to, or admire. Someone you hope to emulate. For your final project you will write an essay and give an in-depth presentation on this person, giving us much more information than you have in your textbook. You will present this person to us in such a way that when we leave the classroom, we feel this person has become our friend."

"Hey, Abe Lincoln, wanna share your lunch?" said Dustin. The back rows burst into snickers again, but not for too long. This was Ms. Trepky's class, after all.

I could picture Abe Lincoln, at some afterlife podium, giving Dustin a sad and stern frown. And then probably half of his sandwich, too, since he was a nice guy.

"Your presentation can have, if you choose, a creative component," Ms. Trepky continued. "This could be a poem, song, piece of art, a dance, whatever you choose. This creative component, or however you choose to present your chosen historical figure, will demonstrate what important things you feel you have learned by spending the semester researching this individual."

Dustin Pierce raised his hand. A rare occurrence. "Can we make a movie?"

"Yes, you may," said Ms. Trepky. Dustin high-fived the pudgy boys on either side of him.

Then it was my turn to raise my hand. I like to know about each assignment as far in advance as possible, so I can plan and prepare, and so I know how much time it's going to take. "What will next semester's project be?"

Ms. Trepky looked down at her hands and there was a flicker at the corner of her mouth that might have been a smile, although I didn't think I'd said something funny. Then I heard the whispers behind me, and even though I couldn't quite hear what they were saying because I don't hear so great, they reminded me that probably nobody else cared about next semester's project already. I thought I maybe heard Dustin mumbling something that started with an *F*, which is the first letter of the name he used to call me. Or maybe they weren't talking about my question at all. It didn't matter. I looked back at Ms. Trepky.

"Next semester's project will be the same, except you will select someone *not* found in our textbook," she said.

I knew immediately who my presentation would be about next semester. Choosing someone *not* in our book was going to be even easier than choosing a textbook person, because I'd already started studying. I'd been reading about my person since I'd first heard her mentioned in a documentary on the National Geographic channel (the channel I always watch whenever I stay home sick). That's the way you learn about things they *don't* teach you in school, everything from vampire squid to this scientist from the early twentieth century. Her name was Cecilia Payne-Gaposchkin. She was an astronomer.

"What?" Dustin said. "But how do we know who to study if they're not in the textbook?"

Ms. Trepky put her hands behind her back. "You have vast resources available to you, Mr. Pierce, including the internet and, dare I say it, the library." She put a hand on our textbook. "In fact, this project is inspired by a real-life scenario. The Smithsonian

Institution in Washington, DC, is hosting a contest, where students from all over the country write a letter about a lesser-known or underrated woman from American science history. They're creating a Women in STEM exhibit, with wax figures representing the underrated women. For the purposes of this class, I think it's a valuable exercise to research those whose contributions to our society are equally as important as the contributions of those who might get more acclaim."

I put the clicking-end of my pen between my teeth. The wax figure of Cecilia was beautiful in my mind, and I could see her smooth, dark hair and pale, piercing eyes. Writing a letter about her would be totally easy. I looked around at the other kids, wondering who they'd pick from outside our textbook. *We're already a step ahead, aren't we, Cecilia? What would you think of bringing in star-shaped Rice Krispies Treats for the presentation?* I could imagine those clear eyes twinkling in response.

Dustin opened his mouth, probably to complain again, and I opened mine to ask if seventh graders were allowed to submit a letter to the Smithsonian contest, but right then there was a knock on the classroom door. It was Ms. Lopez, the principal, and she had a girl with her. The girl had a round face and the longest, thickest hair I had ever seen. She would be the tallest, and I thought the most beautiful, person in our class.

I rolled my pen around my desk, smiling. How many wonderful surprises could fit in one day?

"Excuse me, Ms. Trepky," said Ms. Lopez. "May I interrupt for a second?"

"Please, come in," Ms. Trepky said, and stepped behind her desk.

Ms. Lopez brought the girl to the front of the room. "This is Talia Latu," she said. She said it with the LI emphasized, like TaLEEuh. Not TAH-lia. "She'll be in Ms. Trepky's homeroom with many of you, and in this History class. Please make sure she feels as welcome as you'd hope to be."

Lucky for me, I was in Ms. Trepky's homeroom, so that meant two classes with this new girl.

"We are excited to have you in our class," said Ms. Trepky. The only open desk in the room was the one next to me, and Ms. Trepky motioned to it. "Please take a seat," she said.

For a moment I was worried Ms. Trepky would assign Talia some kind of buddy or partner. Working with partners made my stomach flutter, because I always ended up worrying more about being a fun partner than about actually doing the assignment. I shouldn't have stressed about it, though. Ms. Trepky simply made sure Talia was settled and had her materials, and then kept on with the lesson. She did ask Talia and me to swap phone numbers, so Talia could call someone if she needed help understanding her catch-up work or something, but that was it. I should have known. Ms. Trepky knew we were in seventh grade, not third.

Later, when the bell rang, Ms. Trepky spoke over the jostle and bustle of packing students. "Ms. Latu, if you will come see me for a moment or two, I will catch you up on the latest assignments. And Ms. Monroe." I stopped. She was looking at me down her long nose. "I suggest rereading the section on Eleanor Roosevelt. There's a quote there you might find interesting."

After History it was lunchtime, and I took my cheese-and-pepperoni sandwich into the library. I eat lunch in the library a lot. The librarian is Mr. Duncan, a smiling old man with deep copper, ashy-knuckled hands that always pat the top of the stack of books he hands me like it's a treasure, and I suppose it is. I don't know if eating lunch in the library is against the rules, but he never makes me leave.

In the library, there's a sign above the door with cartoon stars with big silly faces, and it says BRIGHTEN YOUR MIND WITH A BOOK. Real stars don't have five points like the cartoon stars, though. They're balls, big burning balls of fire. I wonder if we made up those five-pointed stars because then it looks like stars have a head and two arms and two legs, like we do. That's the kind of thing I think about when I eat lunch in the library.

A library as your best friend is great, but it *does* have some downsides. I can't text the library. I can't tell it the joke my dad told me about how the paramecium crossed the road because it was stuck to the chicken's butt. I can't go with it to parties, and it's not someone for me to talk to in the crowd.

Last year, one of the teachers asked me who my best friend at school was. I had a friend in third grade who would sometimes come over to play, but she moved away the next year. I told him that my new best friend was probably the library. It doesn't even bother me to read about spinal fluid or fungus (or sometimes Eleanor Roosevelt, who actually seems pretty cool) while I eat. When I told my teacher that he looked at me for a moment with a sort of sad-ish face, almost like he was going to pat me on the head, and then he told me I should try playing outside with the other kids at lunch. That's what made me realize maybe I shouldn't tell people that the library is my best friend.

Even though it is.

Home Is Where the Bach Is

You can tell a lot about a family by the very first thing you see when you walk in their front door. Maybe it's a photo of their dog. Maybe it's an overflowing coat closet with muddy boots poking through the doors.

When you walk into my house, the first thing you see is my mother's Steinway concert grand piano. My mom once had a full-ride scholarship to Juilliard. She even played in Carnegie Hall. Then she got nerve damage in her left hand.

It took her a long time, she told me, to find a new dream, but she realized that, like in music, you can say silent, special things to people with cakes and cookies. I'm not exactly sure what she means, because how can you say things to people without actually, you know, saying them? Anyway, she discovered that an only half-useful left hand doesn't hold you back as much in a kitchen as it does on a piano keyboard. She's even figured out how to manage most of the cake decorating with only her right hand, and she has an assistant at her bakery who helps, too.

She still likes to play piano sometimes, but she gets frustrated when her left hand won't do what she wants it to. She especially loves to play when my big sister, Nonny, is here. Mom can play the right hand if Nonny can do the left.

Both Mom and Nonny won a piano contest called the Colorado State Young Musicians contest when they were twelve. When they were my age.

I always wanted to win the Colorado State Young Musicians contest when I was twelve.

I wanted to be Mom's left hand, too.

But here's the thing about music and me.

There's something that happens to my muscles when I look at piano music. It starts in my shoulders, then spreads down my arms and to my gut. My shoulders become stiff and hard to move, and my hands get cold, and I suddenly have to pee really bad.

Sometimes people talk about deer in headlights

like it's a cliché, but I read about it once in a magazine, and it's very scientific. Adrenaline floods their body and literally makes their muscles freeze even though a big old truck's about to blam right into them. I think maybe when my brain looks at piano music, it turns into a stupid, frightened baby deer that only sees an oncoming big-rig.

I really tried. For three years I took piano lessons, complete with frozen-brain practicing sessions and one especially jaw-clenching recital that totally flopped. So when I was ten I finally quit.

Afterward, when I wasn't turned to stone on the piano bench anymore, I sometimes talked to Beethoven and Bach in my head, asking them why they had to make it so hard for people like me. Sometimes it felt like they looked down at me in their white wigs, pointed their fingers, and laughed.

Nonny is really good at music.

I don't think Beethoven and Bach laugh at *her*.

You might think this means that I'm jealous of Nonny because she can do all these things I can't do. Not just piano. She can also help Mom in the kitchen without breaking bowls or messing things up. And she can do the monkey bars. I've never been able to do the monkey bars.

Let me tell you the truth about Nonny.

Nonny is my safe person.

She's the person I can talk to who never makes me feel like I've said the wrong thing. She's even better and more helpful to talk to than the people in my head. Of course, my parents are also good to talk to. They never make me feel dumb when I say things, but they still sometimes get that look like I'm *so precious* or *growing up so fast*. I'm still their little girl, you know?

Then there's my sister, Nonny.

Her real name is Naomi, but I couldn't say it when I was little, and so now everyone calls her Nonny. She's twenty, almost nine years older than me, but she doesn't talk to me like I'm her baby sister. She has long, long dark hair and a clear complexion pale as starlight, and she's married to a man named Thomas who has the best laugh and the broadest shoulders and can still lift me over his head with one arm. He's got deep, night-sky skin, what Nonny calls a wrinkly-eyed Idris Elba smile, and he once beat my dad at Boggle, which is super hard to do. They met last fall, at Nonny's first semester away at college. They fell in love fast, like gravity pulling two moons into orbit around each other, and then got married in May, right before the end of the school year. And right before Nonny's twentieth birthday. I think my parents were really nervous about her getting married so young, except then we met Thomas. Then they weren't nervous.

Let me tell you a story about my sister.

A couple of years ago, during Nonny's senior year of high school, I got hearing aids. I didn't know that kids at school would think they were weird until after I got them. Nobody made fun of me or anything. Then at the beginning of last year when I was on the playground at lunch I started talking to these two girls with bangle bracelets up both their arms, and they were nice but after a few minutes one of them said, "Sorry, I'm not really used to playing with people who wear hearing aids." They went over to the swings and I went and ate my lunch in the library.

Want to know the weird part? I didn't even feel bad about it. At least not at first. I just thought, *Okay*, and I went and read a book about the discovery of penicillin. (Penicillin was an accident, by the way.)

When I got home, though, I had more time to think about what had happened. That wasn't so good. I didn't cry or anything, but when I was done with my homework I couldn't think of anything to do except sit on my bed and feel very, very small. Sometimes you feel like you could shout and scream so loud your lungs would burst, and to the rest of the world it would only be about as loud as a mosquito fart.

Then Nonny came home from school. She came in and said hello to me, and she could tell that I wasn't having the greatest day ever, and then I told her what had happened and she paused for a moment, but not for too long, and said, "Wow, they must not know very many interesting people at all."

Then she brought me into her room and we blasted Celtic Woman (her favorite) and danced around with hairbrush microphones.

You may not think that Celtic Woman is good blasting-dancing music.

If you think that, let me tell you something.

You're wrong.

Especially if you're singing with Nonny.

X's and O's

There are a few reasons I'm different from Nonny. A few reasons why piano doesn't work out so well for me. Why I'll always be shorter than her, why my heart was ballooned up way too big when I was born, and why I have to wear hearing aids.

It's sort of a big bundle of crazy, chaotic, dangerous weirdness that happened when I was born.

You ready for this?

Here it goes.

Picture this:

1. The big tube of blood in your heart—it's called the aorta—squeezed, pinched, and constricted so blood can't get through and your heart has

to pound harder and harder, growing bigger and bigger until it's ready to pop like some cheesy love song.

2. Your small intestines in a sack outside your stomach where your belly button is supposed to be, and the doctor carefully pushing them back into place. (Gross, but also kind of totally awesome.)

3. The umbilical cord wrapping tighter and tighter around your neck like a boa constrictor.

Fun times, right? When I was two weeks old they took me in for heart surgery, stretching my arms up above my head so they could go in under my ribs instead of cracking open a two-week-old sternum. I always imagine it like some kind of medieval torture. I still have the long white scar across my left side from where they fixed my heart.

Wanna know *why* my heart was squeezed like a cat's head in a toilet-paper tube?

Here's how Mom and Dad explained it to me when I was seven years old.

It's like your body is a recipe cooked in your mom's belly. (I know what a uterus is now, but when I was seven and we were in the middle of a restaurant, they called it a belly.) The Recipe of

You has forty-six ingredients. Those ingredients are called *chromosomes*.

Red hair? Chromosomes. Bad eyesight? Chromosomes. A nose like your great-grandpa Stan's? All thanks to chromosomes.

You get twenty-three ingredients from your dad, and twenty-three from your mom, and together those ingredients make up the Recipe of You. There are two special chromosomes that mean you're born male or female, and you get one of them from your mom and one from your dad.

Except when you don't.

The two female chromosome ingredients are XX. That means your mom is XX, and so when you get your twenty-three mom ingredients, you get one of her X's.

Male ingredients are XY. That means it's your dad's ingredients that decide if you're born male or female. Here's how it works. Y is the "male" ingredient. Since Dad is XY, if he gives you an X, you get one X from Dad, one X from Mom, and *boom bam*, XX, you're a girl. If Dad gives you a Y instead, though, then you've got X from Mom, Y from Dad, and XY, happy birthday, it's a boy.

But it doesn't always work out like that.

Sometimes you're just X.

One X and something's missing.

XO.

Which doesn't stand for hugs and kisses.

It stands for Missing Ingredient.

It doesn't bother me too much. In fact, some people who are called boys or girls when they're born decide that, actually, that word and all its associations doesn't suit them after all. But I've always felt like a girl, all the way from my head to my toes. So I once asked my mom if having only one X meant I might be a boy—and she said it's not like that, because I don't have the Y "male" ingredient, and plus I don't feel like a boy at all. That means I'm just as much a girl as she is.

Here are some more facts: 1 in every 2,500 girls is born XO.

This is called Turner syndrome.

Sometimes when a baby is getting made and the mom's body senses that it's missing an ingredient, her body stops making the baby and it dies before it's even born. That's called a miscarriage. A miscarriage happens to 99 percent of babies who are being made with a missing ingredient.

That means I'm really lucky.

Dad says it means I'm meant to be here.

There are lots of other ways things can go wonky

with the ingredients. For example, it's also possible to get an *extra* chromosome. An extra number-twenty-one ingredient from Mom or Dad. That is called Down syndrome.

Maybe it's miraculous anybody is born "healthy" at all. A miraculous protostar bursting out of a perfect mix of dust and heat.

Turner syndrome fiddles with my body in some ways. Like my ballooned-up heart.

Like my neck that's a bit thick on the sides.

Like my ribs that are round like a barrel.

Like my low-set ears that don't hear exactly perfectly.

Like how I have to give myself shots every day.

But that's just physical stuff. My brain is still intact.

I'm still going to get an A in Biology.

I'm still going to be a scientist.

Better Than a Puppy

Ready for the surprise?

Want to know what's better than a puppy?

I practically burst through the school doors after the last bell rang, and Mom was there waiting for me in the pickup zone. She knew I wouldn't be doing any slowpoking today. (Although I'm not ever really what you could call a slowpoke. Mom says I'm a human espresso. Well, I espressoed my way to the van, that's for sure.)

I yanked open the back door. "So it's time to go get my new puppy, right?"

Mom laughed. "You'll see. Wait till we get home."

I admit, I had my suspicions that the surprise had something to do with my sister. Mom and Nonny had been talking on the phone a lot lately.

Like, *seriously* a lot. There was almost no day that I didn't come out from school and see Mom talking on her phone while she waited for me. And I knew it was Nonny she was talking to, because I could tell by the way she gestured with her hands, and sometimes I would open the car door and hear her say something like, "Love you, too, sweetheart," or once I heard her say, "Let me know how the appointment goes."

I also knew their phone calls had something to do with Thomas's job. He does special welding for big projects, and a couple of months ago the company he worked for had to lay off lots of people. Thomas was one of them, which makes me think that the company wasn't very smart because Thomas was definitely their best guy. He'd been trying to get another job but it wasn't working out so well.

I had asked Mom about fifty times what was going on, but Mom kept saying she'd talk to me about it later. I hate later. Later is the worst.

But maybe Later was finally Now.

Mom usually had splotches of sugar or flour on her clothes somewhere, because she always came straight to my school from the bakery, and she usually went back for a couple of hours before dinner. Today she didn't. Today she was clean.

"Tell me! Tell me!" I said.

Mom grinned. "You'll see."

When you don't know when Later is coming it sucks, but knowing that it's almost here and that it's getting closer and closer is wonderful and exciting, and being excited is the best feeling in the world.

It had been an exciting day.

On the drive home, a drive I'd done millions of times before, every tree seemed new and beautiful. Every house seemed important, like the person who would figure out how to cure cancer could be living inside it.

And when we got home, there was the surprise, waiting for me on the front steps, her big-sister arms open wide enough to jump into.

My Sister Is Sick and It's a Good Thing

"I'm sorry I wasn't there to pick you up," Nonny said when we were inside on the couches. We each had herbal tea and orange marmalade toast and I don't think I'd ever felt so warm and snuggly on the inside. "I was already feeling carsick and wasn't even in a car."

"Carsick? Are you okay? Is Thomas here, too? How long are you staying?"

Nonny laughed and Mom stroked my hair. Here are the answers they gave to my questions:

1. Nonny would be staying for six months. *Six months.* When they told me that I nearly bounced off the couch.

2. Thomas was not here. Yesterday he had flown from their apartment in Chicago (where his parents also lived) to a job doing some crazy project in the Florida Keys. Nonny said it wasn't his favorite job but he had to take it because they needed the money. They were trying to save up for a house. He would be gone for nearly six months before that job ended and he'd have to find a new one. Nonny told me that last night by herself was the worst night of her life.

3. She was okay. She sometimes felt a little nauseated, but that was to be expected.

4. Expected, because she was pregnant.

"*Pregnant!*" I said. "A baby? A real-life baby? This is the best day of my whole life! Six months, holy cow . . . but . . . oh my goodness."

A baby.

Nonny was going to have a baby.

My mom and dad were going to be a grandma and grandpa.

Nonny was going to be the greatest mom.

I was going to be an aunt.

"Yep," Nonny said. She was smiling clear up to her eyes, and even though she looked a bit tired, she proved that pregnancy-glow thing was real. Total glow.

"Tell her more," Mom said. "Tell her when." Mom was practically glowing, too. I thought her face was going to break, she was grinning so wide.

"Well," Nonny said, looking at me. "I'm four months along, and the baby is due February seventeenth." She looked down at her stomach. "That's the other reason Thomas had to take this job. So I'll need your help taking care of me since Thomas isn't here."

I was going to take care of my sister and her unborn child. I had maybe never heard anything so wonderful in my whole life.

Nonny looked at Mom. "I still . . . I mean, I got pregnant so much quicker than we thought. Thank goodness for online classes so school isn't stalled entirely. The timing, though . . . I mean, I really hope they'll let him off for a good chunk of time when the baby's born, even if he has to go back. For a couple weeks, though, he won't be here." She looked back at me. "But you'll take care of things."

"Yes," I said, my fists clenched tight because I could hardly hold my body together. "Yes, yes, I will."

Nonny smiled, then laid her head back on the couch and closed her eyes. Mom gave her That Look, that Too Precious to Handle look, and I admit it, it was actually nice to see that none of us ever grew out of being her little kids, no matter how old or married or pregnant we got.

How pregnant Nonny got, rather. That one would only ever be her.

There's an app on my phone called Marco Polo that Mom let me download especially so I can send video messages to Thomas, and I sent one then. "She's here!" I said. "She made it! Everyone say hi to new dad Thomas!"

He sent a message right back, his hard hat on and his face sweaty. "My main people! Aw, I miss you guys. Thanks for the chat, Lobster. Keep me updated on you-know-who, mmkay?"

(Yeah, he calls me Lobster. Let's just say the first time he came to meet the family we went out to a seafood restaurant and there was an incident involving my dinner still having eyeballs.)

I looked at my sister while her eyes were closed. She didn't look pregnant. Except for the glow. I decided I should watch her very carefully in the next few months. Maybe I should document the experience. Track when her ankles started swelling. Track how big her belly slowly grew. Track when the morning sickness went away. Go with her to doctor's visits, if she'd let me.

Otherwise, I'd never know what it was like.

A Shot a Day Makes the Doctor Say Yay

Not very many twelve-year-old girls have to give themselves shots every day, but really it's not bad at all.

Sometimes Turner syndrome messes with your heart. (It messed with mine pretty good.) Sometimes Turner syndrome messes with your thyroid or your kidneys. (Mine? So far, so good.) But there are two things that Turner syndrome *always* does:

1. Turner syndrome means you can't have babies of your own. Nonny's taking care of that one for our family, and I don't even need to think about that right now anyway. Right?
2. Turner syndrome means you don't grow to a normal height. Not on your own, anyway. But

there's special medicine called growth hormone and if you give yourself a shot of that stuff every day for a while, you can do a pretty fine job with the whole growing thing. I'm already over five feet tall. Without the shots I'd barely pass four.

I'm pretty lucky, actually. Since my doctors figured out about my Turner syndrome stuff soon after I was born, that meant I got to start shots early and do plenty of growing. Sometimes girls with Turner syndrome don't find out until it's too late for the shots.

The needles don't scare me. They're small. My bedtime supplies aren't *that* different from everyone else's. Toothbrush, pajamas, needle. Check, check, check.

Mom used to give me the shots. Then I told her I wanted to learn how to do it on my own, and after she taught me, I did it in one try.

In one shot. Ha-ha.

Easy as brushing your teeth.

(Okay, sometimes Mom still helps with my shots if I'm doing the shot in a place I can't reach, like my shoulder or my *gluteus maximus*, which is a noun meaning: butt.)

My big, tough, blowtorch wielding brother-in-law,

Thomas, can work with flames and dangerous buzzing tools inches from his face no problem, but needles? Total heebie-jeebies. It still makes me laugh when I think about his face the first time he saw me do my shots.

The thing is, though, shots don't make me feel brave because they're not even scary. It's only medicine. A little pinch. Done.

For other people, maybe shots *are* scary. Thomas once told me if he's around needles it's hard for him to be brave. But then, he doesn't need to be brave about talking to new people and making friends. Even at a really hard job, the annoying people he works with end up his friends, and grumpy old bosses turn out to like him a lot. I remember once when he visited and we went out as a family he talked to the waiter at our table and the ticket taker at the movie theater like they'd known each other all their lives. Like they're best friends. I don't know how he does that.

Nonny says when he asked her out for the first time, he wasn't shy or awkward at all. If a boy ever asked me on a date (when I'm forty-two, like Dad says) I would definitely need to be brave. Even lab partners give me butterflies.

It's not that I'm shy. I'm really not. I get A's on all my class presentations, and I think doing high school drama will be really fun. Talking to people isn't the hard part. It's that I can never tell what people think is the wrong thing to say until after I've said it.

Like asking Ms. Trepky about homework that isn't due for more than six months.

Or telling a teacher about my bestie, the library.

Me trying to figure out who to talk to at a birthday party?

I'd rather stick a needle in my butt.

Growth Hormone
and Marmalade

We stayed up too late. We basically *must* stay up late when Nonny's home.

Mom used to make marmalade toast when we were sick, and it's especially great on her fresh, homemade bread. Mom, Nonny, and I sat at the table in the kitchen eating too much toast.

Mom took a sip of her tea. Nonny took a sip. Nonny rubbed the table with the sleeve of her sweater, wiping up the wet ring from her mug. Maybe watching people drink herbal tea sounds boring but I could have stayed up watching them forever.

"You've got school in the morning, sweetie," Mom said.

"And I'll drive you," Nonny said.

"Deal!" I said.

Mom finished the last bite of her toast. "I know you want to stay up but it's time to start getting ready for bed."

Right then Dad sashayed into the kitchen, blaring Beyoncé's "Run the World" from his phone. He pulled Nonny up from her seat and twirled her, and she nearly bumped her nose into his armpit. I laughed so hard I snorted. Even though Nonny had told Dad the special news a couple of weeks ago, while the adults were coordinating her coming home and everything, having Nonny actually here meant he'd been distracted from lesson planning all night long.

"You are ridiculous," Mom said.

"I was thinking," Dad said, "that even though we don't know the sex yet, and nothing changes how perfect my new grandbaby is going to be . . . Wouldn't it be great to have a baby girl in the family again?"

He grabbed my hand and tried to twirl Nonny and me in some kind of knot-windmill move but we ended up crashing into each other and laughing.

"Okay, okay, you sillies," Mom said. "A couple of you really do have school tomorrow."

"Do I hafta?" Dad said.

I went to the pantry where we kept peanut butter (for Dad), Chips Ahoy! (for Nonny), and a box of sterilized needles (for me). Then I got the small vial of medicine from the fridge. The vials aren't any bigger than my dad's thumb.

"I haven't watched you do this in a while," Nonny said. "I'm still really impressed."

"Impressive is in her genes," Dad said.

Nonny flinches when she watches me do my shots. I think she's just a tiny bit afraid of needles.

I unwrapped the needle from its paper packaging and took off the long plastic cap. There was the tiny little needle.

"Tell us your Hard Reading Words while you do it," Mom said, "and then bed."

Holding the needle was as normal to me now as holding a pencil. I pushed the sharp tip into the rubbery top of the bottle.

"*Flabbergast*," I said. "It means to shock or amaze. *Perturbed* means annoyed."

I tipped the bottle so the clear liquid inside poured down to the top, where the needle was. This watery liquid was my growth hormone, the medicine that made me grow as tall as other girls. Dad calls it my Magic Beanstalk Juice.

"*Implore* means to beg and beg."

Very carefully I pulled the plunger part down and down until the growth hormone filled the syringe to the exact right line.

"*Antagonize* means to be mean or a bully."

I pulled the syringe out of the bottle and held it up close to my eyes to make sure there were no bubbles. I gently flicked the syringe a couple of times, like Mom showed me, to make double sure. I lifted my shirt just a little bit until I could see my belly button and I pinched a bit of my tummy pudge.

"And *persist* means to keep going and going, no matter what."

Then bam. Poke the needle fast into the pinched bit of tummy, push in the Magic Beanstalk Juice slow like testing out a peach with your thumb, then pull the needle out.

Easy peasy.

"Didn't hurt?" Nonny asked.

"Nope," I said.

"Man oh man," she said. "I think when they give my baby immunizations I'm going to cry louder than the baby. And I hope . . . I really hope we're out of this dumb financial black hole before—"

"Don't worry," Mom said. "You'll both figure something out. And we're here to help."

"I remember when you guys got your first shots," Dad said. "And *I* was the one who ended up needing a juice box from the nurse."

I thought about the baby in its brand-new diaper, with the tiny black raisin belly button still stuck on its stomach from the umbilical cord. I thought about the baby getting shots. Immunizations— normal shots. For a tiny baby, new to the world and not used to pricking needles, that would be bad enough.

But what if the baby needed different kinds of shots?

I knew better than most that needing shots could mean other things. Could mean much worse, something-got-messed-up things.

What if the baby needed shots like mine?

Not very many twelve-year-old girls have to give themselves shots every day. Nonny's baby being one of them would hurt worse than getting the shots myself.

Much worse.

Back in my room, I thought about Nonny's face when she was talking about a financial black hole. I hadn't really noticed that she seemed a tiny bit scared until she said it out loud.

My history book poking out of my backpack

made me think of the contest Ms. Trepky had mentioned. I hadn't gotten a chance to ask her about sending in a letter of my own, but I decided to look up the contest and see for myself.

At my computer, I fast-typed *Smithsonian Women in STEM contest* and clicked through to the contest page.

Exactly like Ms. Trepky had said, it was a contest based on writing letters about underrated female scientists from history. The letters were supposed to be about how that special scientist and the spectacular things they'd accomplished had impacted the world, and then how she had impacted or inspired you in your own life. That was the first part. Then in the last part of the letter, you were to tell a story about something you had done to teach people about the scientist, to raise awareness. The deadline for the contest was Valentine's Day, so I had months to do my awareness project and write my letter.

For this contest, Cecilia would work *perfectly*. The contest had three divisions—eleventh/twelfth grade, ninth/tenth grade, and seventh/eighth grade—which meant that I, Libby Monroe, could enter. I just had to write the most perfect, well-crafted letter, and come up with the most spectacular project idea to teach people about Cecilia. Each contest division would have a winner who would receive a plaque and five thousand dollars for their school.

And then there was the grand prize.

What that one grand-prize winner would win almost made me spill my drink in my lap.

Ready for this?

The grand-prize winner of the Smithsonian Institution's Women in STEM contest would win twenty-five thousand dollars.

That's right. *Twenty-five thousand dollars.*

That's twenty-five with three zeros after it, for them to use however they want. *Plus* another twenty-five thousand, for their school, which made it even more unbelievably spit-take, drink-spillingly mind-blowing.

But twenty-five thousand dollars. I knew exactly what I'd do with it, too. Because twenty-five thousand dollars is enough money even in adult terms for a down payment on a house your sister and her husband are trying to save up for.

I couldn't be Mom's left hand. I couldn't be a mother the way Nonny would be.

But if I worked hard enough, I *could* calm that financial black hole in Nonny's mind.

I could help bring Thomas home, so he wouldn't have to take any more faraway jobs.

Kids sometimes weren't the very nicest, and sometimes that would remind me that I had a scarred heart and missing chromosomes and didn't play any of the games in PE very well. If I could do this one humongous thing, though, this biggest of all accomplishments, then maybe I'd have that inside me like hot herbal tea and warm marmalade toast no matter what cold words anybody else said. Even if nobody else knew what I could do, I would know.

Sometimes in my brain, an idea arrives huge and round and blocks out most everything else, like an eclipse. I could feel this idea of the contest, of helping Nonny, doing exactly that. Mom knows my mind works this way sometimes and calls it my tunnel vision. She knows I can get too focused on something when it's so bright in my mind's eye it's like the sun, that one idea shining its own light over all the rest. But winning this contest and helping Nonny? Yeah, that could be my sun for a while.

I could do it. I had to.

Silent Questions

With Nonny staying, I decided to try talking to some new people at school. If it didn't go super great, like last time, Nonny and I always had Celtic Woman to cheer me up. And my new secret mission made me feel braver, somehow.

At lunch I brought my peanut butter sandwich to a table with some new girls. One girl had the NASA logo on her T-shirt, so they seemed like they would be fun to eat lunch with. They smiled when I sat down, which was good. I told them my name and they each told me theirs. The girl in the NASA shirt was named Charise.

We talked about classes and then I talked about my sister and her piano and how beautiful her wedding was and also about my mom's bakery.

"She makes these special cupcakes with dark purple frosting and white sprinkles and it makes them look like constellations," I said.

"Oh."

"One time I was helping her make the cupcakes and my grandma had given us this big ceramic yellow bowl that we keep apples in and I was moving it to make room on the counter and then I dropped it and it totally broke."

"Oh no," they said.

"But you guys should come try those cupcakes sometime. They're really good. You can get chocolate or vanilla flavored."

"Okay."

It seemed to me like everything was going great until they finished eating and picked up their lunches and left.

It was okay. I ate my sandwich by myself. I guess I ate even faster because without other people I wasn't talking so much. Except to Cecilia Payne, in my head. *If we can figure out the stars, then why are other people so confusing?* I didn't hear an answer, but a narrow square of sunlight coming in through the lunchroom blinds sat in the seat across from me.

When I got home from school, Nonny set a plate of marmalade toast on the coffee table in the front room, next to the papers she was reading for her new online college classes. ("Thank goodness for scholarships and supportive career counselors," she'd said.) She was on the phone, holding it up against her ear with her shoulder, but she'd made toast especially for me. I wasn't sick, but I sure needed some marmalade toast.

I got out my math book while Nonny was on the phone. I worked on my worksheet while Nonny said "hmm," and "oh wow." The other person was telling some kind of story. Sitting on the couch listening to her made me feel like I'd taken a time machine back to when she was in high school. She talked to people on the phone a lot back then, the same way she did now. Like dozens of people knew that she was the one to call when they had questions or problems, and after they talked to her everything was a little better.

Nonny didn't say very much herself. Sometimes she asked a question. The words she *did* use always seemed to be exactly right, like they were some kind of magic healing spell.

How did she learn to say those perfect magic-spell words? Maybe it was the questions she asked? Or was there a special way she told the other person she was listening?

Nonny stayed quiet for a long time, and I thought maybe that was part of the spell. She did something in her mind when she was quiet, some special way of thinking or listening, and that made her know the right words to say when she finally said them. There had to be a way to learn her trick, whatever it was.

Most days I'm super-good at doing my homework right away, but today I listened to her instead of focusing on my math. After she said goodbye to the person on the phone, she put her cell in her back pocket, and came and sat by me on the couch.

"So how did the genius do at school today?" she asked.

Of course, I didn't have the right words to answer, so instead I took a bite of toast. Nonny knows how to do toast perfectly, where the bread is the exact right level of crispiness, and the marmalade is spread thick over each crumb and corner.

Nonny waited for me to finish my bite and answer.

"It wasn't my ultimate best day ever or anything," I said.

She tucked her hair behind her ear and settled into the couch, looking at me. She waited again.

"I . . . I tried sitting by some new people at lunch today," I said. "One girl was wearing a NASA shirt. She was cool. Her name was Charise."

"Good for you!" Nonny said.

"I don't know about that," I said.

"Yeah?" she said.

"I think maybe they're already friends together," I said.

Nonny put her arm on the back of the couch and her long hair spread over her shoulder like a waterfall. She kept watching me, waiting for when I was ready with the right words. Sometimes it really was easier to sit with a square of sunlight or talk to the spirit of a great astronomer than people in real life. At least then I never said the wrong thing.

"Were you talking to a friend?" I said. "On the phone? I remember you had a lot of friends at school."

"I like talking to people," Nonny said. "Especially you."

"What do they talk to you about?" I said. "I mean, you're so smart about it. It's like talking to you is magic and then they're happy again."

Nonny laughed. "I don't know about magic," she said.

I was already feeling better simply being with her, so I knew Nonny had some kind of magic no matter what she said. "Oh, come on, tell me the secret spell."

"No spell, but I guess there's something I do in my head. Kind of a trick maybe?"

"A trick?"

"It's sort of a trick for having lunch with new people, but it works for people you already know, too."

I took a sip of tea and put the mug down. I wanted to pay attention to this. "And this is why people are always calling you? Like your friends always calling and asking you for advice?"

Nonny did a quiet smile. It's easier for me when I think of quiet smiles or loud smiles. It makes it easier to know what the smile means.

"Maybe," she said.

I crossed my legs and faced her. "Tell me the trick!"

"Well," she said. "You know how sometimes you want to get to know somebody, and it's hard to know what to ask them? And maybe it's easier to talk about things you know, because they might know about those things, too?"

I almost choked on my toast. That was exactly what had happened with Lunch Table Girls.

"That happens for you, *too*?" I asked.

"Then there's times when someone is telling you about something really difficult they're going through and you're not quite sure what to say? When you're pretty positive nothing you say will help or make anything any better?"

I realized I was twisting the hem of my pants without noticing. This wasn't something I'd talked a lot about before, not even with Nonny. "Even when they're not saying hard things it's sometimes like I always say the wrong thing back."

"Oh Libby," Nonny said. She put a hand on my knee. "Sometimes it's hard to know what to say, or sometimes there are too many things to say. I know you always have fifty questions for everyone, and everything, and maybe it's hard to know what to say *because* there's so much."

I nodded.

"When that happens, the trick is sort of asking them the question in my mind. I ask one or maybe even all fifty of the questions that you probably have, but I only ask them silently, in my head, to the other person."

So it *was* like talking to my scientist friends in my head! Talking to them silently and so never saying the wrong thing because the stars and the universe helped you know the right words. This was exactly the same but with real-life people.

"So it's asking the exactly right question because it's only in your head!" I said. "A Silent Question!"

"Silent Question. I like that," Nonny said, laughing. "That's perfect. And after I ask a Silent Question then yes, exactly, it's almost like the universe itself picks the very best of all the things I'm silently asking or saying in my head, and then the other person keeps talking like I've said or asked just the right thing. Like I'm really hearing them, really listening. My staying silent lets the other person say only the things they want to."

It was like the last puzzle piece in a super-hard thousand-piece Eiffel Tower puzzle clicked into place in my brain. There were silent conversations going on everywhere, between two people, between a person and the universe. And those conversations went two ways. I knew they did, because it had happened to me before. I've made deals with the universe, and with my scientist friends. I talked to them and the universe answered back.

A couple of years ago my mom came back from the doctor looking pale and scared. She and Dad talked for a long time and then brought Nonny and me out to the couch.

Here's a big doctor word for you: *melanoma*.

"They found skin cancer," Mom said. "I'm not going to . . . to lie to you guys, it's a pretty rare kind. They think we caught it in time, though. They said they're ninety-percent sure it's going to be fine."

When it comes to your mom, the only percent fine you want to hear is one-hundred.

They took a long, football-shaped chunk of skin off my mom's shoulder, then sewed it up into a long scar. They also took a few of her lymph nodes.

When Mom went in for surgery, you can bet I talked to the universe.

I talked to the universe for hours and hours. To Rosalind Franklin, specifically, because she was the one I thought could help. She knew about genetics, about cells. So I made a deal with Rosalind

Franklin, and you know what? A month later, Mom was dancing around the bakery, covered in flour.

Silent Questions with people. Silent Deals with the universe. How do people without good teachers and big sisters learn this stuff?

"That is the smartest thing I've heard all day," I said. "And that's saying a lot because we talked about Albert Einstein in school today."

Nonny laughed.

It's my favorite thing, making Nonny laugh.

No Payne, No Gain

Here is what I know about Cecilia Payne:

1. She was the first student, girl or boy, to get a PhD from the Harvard College Observatory, and the first female department chair at Harvard.
2. She was the first person to discover the chemicals and elements inside stars.
3. A professor told her that her research was wrong, and then published the same results four years later. He's the one who got credit for finding out about stars.
4. She is not in my textbook.

That meant she was the perfect person to use for both my second-semester class project *and* the Smithsonian contest. A small, whiny voice in my head kept trying to remind me that I was competing with high school juniors and seniors for that grand prize. That didn't scare me for too long, though, because I knew I would work harder than anyone. I'd write the best letter the Smithsonian people had ever read, and not just for a seventh grader. Then Nonny and Thomas and the new baby would be set. Then, after all these years of Mom and Dad and Nonny helping me, I'd actually be able to give something back. Something great.

If I was going to use Cecilia for my letter, though, and do the most amazing awareness project the Smithsonian had ever seen, there was more to learn. I wanted to test out an idea before moving on to this semester's person.

I flipped open my computer, tapping my toe on the floor out of habit. I put my cup of green grapes next to the computer on my desk. Tippity-tap on the keyboard and pretty soon I was on the Harvard website. Maybe Cecilia wasn't in my textbook, but after hearing about her on the documentary, I wondered what Harvard had to say. I typed in her name in the Harvard website search bar.

Boom. A whole special astronomy lecture series named after Cecilia. That seemed pretty nice of the Harvard people.

I kept looking. I clicked around and found the list of people who have been Astronomy Department chairs at Harvard. And guess what I found out.

There have been seventeen Astronomy Department chairs at Harvard.

Sixteen of them are men.

I think that makes Cecilia even more special.

The Astronomy Department chairs seem like cool guys. I mean, anybody who studies astronomy for their job has to be pretty cool, right? I wondered, though, if more girls would want to study the stars if they knew about Cecilia.

One thing about me—I've had to stay home sick from school a little more often than other girls, but I think it's worth it if it means watching documentaries about the world and the super-cool people in it. Turner syndrome meant I had a higher number of ear infections than most kids and an immune system whose only defense weapon seemed to be a squirt gun, but that was okay. Knowing Cecilia was worth a little flu, any day.

I liked learning and teaching myself cool medical stuff, too, probably because I spend so much time around doctors. Most of that stuff is fascinating, and very good to know. A few things, though, are not so good.

Like how sometimes when a baby is ready to be born, it isn't facing the right way, and the baby and the mommy can get really hurt. Maybe even die. That is called *breech*.

Like how sometimes a baby gets born much, much too early, and it's like taking muffins out of the oven when they're still soupy goopy dough, except with a baby it's things like their heart and lungs and brain that aren't ready. That is called *premature*.

Like how sometimes if the mom's body can tell that there is something wrong with the baby, something like a missing chromosome, it will get rid of the baby on its own. Whether the mom wants to or not. That's that scary word again: *miscarriage*.

Now that there was an actual new baby coming into the family, I couldn't get those things out of my head. I was lying on my bed thinking about my letter and everything I knew about pregnancy and looking at the posters on my wall, and I think that's what gave me the idea.

Everything was converging, and Cecilia was in the middle of it.

It was time for a Universe Deal. The most important deal I'd ever make.

There are two posters next to my bed. One is of

the muscles in the human body. Those are much harder to memorize than bones. The other poster is of the Milky Way.

I could hear Mom and Nonny in the kitchen down the hall, laughing about something. The whole time she'd been here we'd never stopped talking about the baby. She finds out next month if it's a boy or a girl. She and Thomas haven't decided on names yet.

I knew exactly who could help. Cecilia wasn't a biologist, but she took something beautiful and mysterious and figured out each of the beautiful and mysterious things that went into it, and isn't creating a new person the exact same thing? If there was someone on the other side—someone in the afterlife—who could figure out how to keep Nonny's baby perfectly healthy and perfectly safe, maybe it was her. Plus, Cecilia had had kids. Three of them. She knows what it's like.

I knew Cecilia could help me, because the woman who figured out what stars are made of had to be one of the smartest women in the world. She was there in the middle of both of my Big Questions, my answer and my solution to helping Nonny with both her financial black hole and with being sure of a safe, healthy baby.

I walked to my window and looked out at the sky that was still bright and clear and blue. Remember that old song from the movie *Pinocchio*? About wishing on stars? Did you ever wonder where the idea of wishing on stars came from? I looked it up once, and it goes back a long time. A way long time. So it went like this—way back in ancient Greece there was this guy Ptolemy. He wrote about how sometimes the gods got bored doing their normal, godly things and sometimes they would look down from the heavens onto the human, mortal world. And sometimes when they did that, a star would accidentally get knocked loose. So when you saw a shooting star it meant they were looking down on you. It meant they were listening and might possibly grant you your wish.

In the middle of the afternoon I couldn't see any stars, especially shooting stars, but I knew they were there.

Here's what I'm asking for, Cecilia Payne, I thought.

No complications.

No defects.

No missing chromosomes. No extra chromosomes. No syndromes.

I knew Universe Deals went two ways, and I

knew I needed to do something for Cecilia Payne, too. Do something important for her, so she could do something important for me. The most important. It would be like putting something good into the stirring soup of the universe until it swirled and swirled its way back to you. Before, when I made the deal with Rosalind Franklin, I used the papier-mâché projects we were doing in art class. I sculpted a tall, spiraling ladder of DNA. It turned out sort of flaky and droopy, despite working my absolute hardest on it, but I painted Rosalind's name a bunch of times on the inside, like she was holding up the whole thing. And she did. Mom got better.

So what about this time? My history book was at the foot of my bed, open to the page on Eleanor Roosevelt. I'd picked her for my first-semester presentation because I couldn't get that quote that Ms. Trepky had said out of my head, and when I really looked at pictures of Eleanor she seemed a bit odd-looking, just a little, and that made me want to know more about her. I was glad she was in my textbook, so lots of other odd-looking girls could read about her.

That was what I could do for Cecilia, I thought.

And that was what I could do for my Smithsonian Women in STEM contest project.

I will get you in my textbook, I told Cecilia.

What better way to teach people about Cecilia and raise awareness of her work? Ms. Trepky would help me. The contest deadline and the baby's due date were right next to each other, practically on the same day, so if this idea worked it would be like the planets aligning, each one reflecting its light toward us at the same time. I'd get Cecilia into the textbook, then win the Smithsonian grand prize.

That is my promise.

I didn't say it out loud, at least not yet, but that is the promise I made in my head to Cecilia Payne, PhD.

That is the wish I made.

I made the promise, and then my hands felt cold. Seniors had a lot more writing practice than I did, and writing a letter as good as the letters they might write wouldn't be easy. Plus, I didn't even know who made textbooks. Can you call the textbook people? Are there textbook people?

I would have to find out.

Because what if the baby was hurt or sick? What if Nonny got hurt? What if . . .

No, I wasn't even going to think about that. Because I would write the best letter, write it over and over again until it sparkled so bright they couldn't ignore it. They'd read it and see what I saw about Cecilia. And in return Cecilia would make sure Nonny and her baby were fine.

They had to.

Give Nonny a perfect baby, I wished with every nucleus of every cell in my body. *A safe, healthy, undamaged baby*, I wished on every shooting star I or Cecilia might ever have seen, and I bet she saw a lot.

And we will start learning about the woman who discovered what stars are made of.

How Not to Make Friends

When I brought my lunch into the library a few days later, someone was already there. Talia was sitting in the armchair over by the *National Geographic* magazines. That's where I usually sat.

I stopped when I saw her, but she didn't see me. She was leaning back in the chair with her eyes closed, and earbuds in. I took a few steps and when I got closer I could see on her phone a picture of some street art and the name Logic.

When I looked back up at her face she was watching me.

"What's Logic?" I said. "Is it a band?"

She didn't speak for a moment. I realized she didn't look too thrilled about me walking up to her and looking at her phone.

Maybe that wasn't really a socially acceptable thing to do.

So of course I had done it, because I always mess up like that.

Talia sighed and took out one earbud. "He's not a band. He's a rap artist."

"Oh," I said. "I've never heard of him."

Talia's shoulders slumped and she sighed again. "I knew this place would be totally hick."

"So where did you come from?" I asked.

Her hand paused in midair, ready to put her earbud back in, and I realized I'd interrupted her music again and was probably bugging her. Then I realized she'd insulted my hometown. Hick? That didn't seem quite fair. Boulder was a college town, after all.

"San Francisco," she said. "But I'm Samoan, since obviously that's what you were really asking. Now can I listen to my music, please?"

I said, "Oh."

I carried my lunch over to the other side of the room, where the textbooks were.

The Silent Questions! I'd forgotten! And this would have been the perfect opportunity to try it out.

So Libby to go overboard and forget the Silent Questions.

I sighed. Oh well, back to the textbooks.

Textbooks from Knight-Rowell Publishing especially. That's who published my textbook *Survey of Modern America*. I'd been researching.

My history book was the sixth edition. I kind of guessed they wouldn't be able to get Cecilia Payne into *this* edition, but if I could start working with them on getting a new edition published with Cecilia in it, then *that's* what I could write about in my Smithsonian letter.

I had a stack of almost a dozen books in front of me before I remembered I needed to eat my lunch. I pulled out my peanut butter banana sandwich and then saw Talia looking at me.

"Are you reading history books for fun?" she asked.

I looked back at the books at my feet. I mean, it was a little bit fun, but that wasn't the right word.

"It's important," I said.

"Whatever," she said, and put her earbud back in.

Art Show

I did some research on Samoa. Guess what I found out?

Government officials from different areas in Samoa are called *matais*. There are twenty-five thousand *matais* in Samoa, and only five percent are girls. One of the coolest people I've found is a woman who was once the Minister of Communication and Technology in Samoa. Her name is Safuneitu'uga Pa'aga Neri.

There's pretty much not a more spectacular name on the planet.

Other things I found out?

The Samoan islands were made from volcanoes. That means volcanoes under the ocean erupted in huge explosions and then *boom*, Samoa. How marvelous is that? There are places on the islands that are big fields of hard, dried lava.

That night we piled into the car for the high school art show, where Dad's students present their work. They do an opening show and closing show each school year, and it's pretty much a holiday in our family, where we go out to dinner and get ice cream and everything. So on the way to the show I told Dad about someone I'd discovered in my research, a Samoan painter named Fatu Feu'u. He's from a village in Samoa and has paintings in collections all around the world.

Dad showed us around the halls, giving us a tour of his students' artwork like he was a curator at a museum. The students had done a shadow-hands assignment, Dad explained, with charcoal and conté crayon. The works looked almost like cave paintings. Dad took us down the row one by one, talking about how they'd been studying positive and negative space, how the lines weren't drawn, only implied. He called the students his kids, like he always did, and since my dad had so much awesome I didn't mind sharing. He looked as proud as if they'd discovered a new species or conquered Everest.

After the show we went out for our traditional

ice cream excursion. I sent Thomas a Marco Polo of some pictures I'd taken of the artwork, and he responded with a message showing himself holding up a totally terrible stick figure drawing and I laughed so hard I almost choked on my rocky road. Nonny also kept saying thanks to Mom and Dad for taking care of her and buying her ice cream, and I'm pretty sure that financial black hole is always sucking at her thoughts.

I showed Dad some paintings by Fatu Feu'u on my phone. They're colorful patterns like a quilt, with flowers and shapes and sometimes wide-eyed faces popping out. I wondered if Talia had ever heard of the village he was from. Or if, just maybe, her ancestors were from around the same place.

Dad liked the paintings, and thought he could maybe even show them in his art class. Do a pattern assignment, maybe. I told Dad about an art organization that Fatu Feu'u started with some of his friends. Dad said he seemed really cool.

I think so, too.

Seventh-Grade Writing

I thought carefully about what to say to Ms. Trepky about my idea for the Smithsonian contest. I didn't need to tell her about the Universe Deal or the financial black hole, but I knew she could help me write the best letter ever. I knew she'd be willing to help me.

I stayed after class while everybody else packed up and went out for lunch.

"Ms. Trepky?"

Ms. Trepky sat in the chair at her desk and pulled out a book. "What can I do for you, Ms. Monroe?"

I hitched my bag over my shoulder and stood in front of her desk. "I have a question."

"Excellent." She leaned back in her chair.

"It's about what you said about that Smithsonian contest where people do a project and write a letter."

"Yes?"

"I was wondering if . . . well, I was thinking I really want to submit a letter, and was wondering if maybe you could look over it after I write it to help me make it better?"

Ms. Trepky smiled one of her rare smiles. It was an excited smile, not an Aren't You Cute smile. "I would be delighted," she said.

"It's not due until February, but I want to get started on my project *and* my letter now so I can make them the best possible."

"Would you like to start a draft over the weekend and then have me look it over?" she said.

I knew she'd ask the right questions.

"That would be great," I said.

"I'll tell you what," Ms. Trepky said. "If you start working on your letter for the contest, I'll look it over as soon as you're ready. And at the end of the year, if you'd like to turn in your letter to me as well, I'd be more than happy to give you extra credit for class. Not that I expect you'll need it."

"That . . . that would be amazing!" I said, giving

one hop instead of jumping up and down like I wanted to.

Ms. Trepky pulled up the contest instruction page on her computer, then printed it out for me so I'd have a copy of the instructions to look at. I planned to tape them on the wall above my computer. Instructions that were going to solve so much. Fix so many problems.

I put the paper carefully into my backpack and headed for the classroom door. *See, Cecilia*, I said in my head. *I'm already on the job. You're watching, right? You're going to help me out?*

"Libby," Ms. Trepky said. "Speak and write as clearly as you do in my class, and they will listen."

"Thanks," I said.

They better, I thought.

Beach Bum

People like Dustin Pierce don't ignore new students.

I've heard him and his cronies come up with nicknames starting with almost every letter of the alphabet. They work harder on those mean nicknames than on homework, it seems.

They ignore me, usually.

But he didn't use to ignore me.

See, there's another thing that sometimes comes with Turner syndrome, and that's these little brown moles that I have on my arms and legs and even some on my face. Lots of people have brown moles—Marilyn Monroe had a beautiful brown mole on her lip—but sometimes when you have

Turner syndrome you get a bit more spotted than other people.

I used to have one on my chin that the doctors were worried about. So I went to the doctor and he took it off. Want to know how weird and neat it is when the doctor takes a mole off? They did a tiny shot on my chin to make it numb, then he took a sharp scalpel and scraped it right off. They had to go deeper on this one to make sure they got it all because they were worried it might turn into a sun cancer mole one day when I was older, and I even had to get stitches.

Remember how I have a scar around my chest?

Well, I have another very small scar from those stitches.

Dustin had a nickname for me that started with *F*.

He called me FrankenChin.

Dustin and his friends don't call me that as much as they used to, which is good. Because it's not new anymore, and they mostly like finding new people and new nicknames to use.

Sometimes I wonder if other people call me that name, too, but because I don't hear so perfectly I just don't hear them. Maybe if I don't hear them it doesn't matter, right?

After school I went to my locker to pack up my backpack. I kept the paper from Ms. Trepky tucked neatly inside the cover of *Survey of Modern America*.

Talia's locker was two down from mine. Whenever she sat next to me in class I tried to remember to smile at her, but I hadn't talked to her since the library. She always had her earbuds in. She didn't look like she wanted to talk.

But other people were talking to her.

Talking *at* her, really.

Dustin Pierce and his two buddies walked past our lockers while Talia took out her earbuds and stuffed them into her pocket.

"Hey there, beach bum," Dustin said. His buddies snorted and they walked quicker down the hall to their lockers, giggling.

Talia froze, but only for a few seconds. The way her shoulders arched made me think they'd been calling her that name all day long. She let her backpack drop to the ground with a *thump*, and put her shoulders back. She opened her locker.

Dozens and dozens of paper scraps tumbled out of her locker onto the floor, some flipping around in the air before they landed. Dustin and his crew must have stuffed them in through the thin slots at the top of the locker. Talia immediately bent to the floor and started scooping them up.

I knelt next to her to help, and that's when I saw it. They weren't just scraps of paper.

They were pictures.

Pictures of butts.

A hundred pictures of butts. Big butts, too. Gigantic butts with stretch marks and wrinkles.

Talia's face was red, and her mouth a knife-sharp line.

What in the world are you supposed to say to someone when you're kneeling in the hallway, scooping up butts?

We picked up every last picture and crumpled them and threw them in the trash. Talia's face was still stretched tight and if I were Dustin Pierce I'd have been terrified of the way Talia's hand was clenching in a fist.

Sometimes knowing the right thing to say would be really nice. But I didn't know.

I remembered the Silent Questions this time. I thought all the things I wanted to say and ask and put them out into the universe. I wanted to tell Talia that I was on her team. That I was her friend. Was that something people usually said silently?

The Silent Questions helped in my own head. I

knew I was at least trying to say the right thing, and my stomach didn't feel as fluttery. I didn't know how much the Silent Questions were helping Talia. Maybe someone can be too angry to hear the Silent Questions you and the universe are asking them, at least for a while. And I didn't blame her. Not one bit.

Finally I said, "Do you think we should tell someone?"

Talia slammed her locker shut and picked up her backpack. "Don't you dare say one word."

First Draft

I pulled the instruction sheet out of my backpack first thing when I got home and set it on my desk. On my computer I started a list of the things I wanted to talk about in my letter. About Cecilia growing up in England and then moving to the United States. About her kids. About her job at Harvard, and about how she figured out what stars are made of.

The Knight-Rowell Publishing website had a contact form. After working on my list, I zoomed over to their site and started filling in the form. I put in my name, my email, and then I wrote about how I wanted to talk to them about a great idea. An idea I knew they would love. An idea for a new edition of the textbook that would include Cecilia Payne.

Then I held my breath. Click. SEND.

Once I heard back from Knight-Rowell Publishing, the project could officially get started.

The instructions for the contest said that the winners would be contacted one month after the deadline. That meant that next spring, I could be the winner of twenty-five thousand dollars. Nonny could be planning for that house or rent or whatever would help the most. Cecilia would keep Nonny's baby safe. It meant that in March, Nonny could start planning on bringing Thomas home. Instead of *missing* a piece in my own body, I'd *fix* a missing piece in the lives of the people I loved.

I could be that person.

I wanted Nonny and Mom and Dad and, well, everyone, to look at me and see what I could fix, not what I needed to have fixed in me. I wanted it so bad it was like my aorta was constricting again. But not this time. This time: fixer, not fixed.

Just this once.

After I sent Knight-Rowell that email, I tried to go back to working on my letter, but that's when the words started swirling around in my brain. I couldn't focus. I kept seeing something else in my mind that distracted me.

I kept seeing Talia's red face, and the way her shoulders hunched when they called her that name. Hunched like she'd been hit.

The first day they come up with a nickname like that, they think they're so clever. I remember. But they're not. I wanted to tell Talia that.

My brain felt as swirly as the Milky Way mess on my poster. I couldn't figure out the right thing to do in this situation. Talia's sad and mad face wouldn't leave my mind. I could let it go and just keep smiling at her when she sat next to me in history class, but that didn't seem like nearly enough. Something needed to be done. Something big, so she'd know she wasn't alone. Something so that we'd be friends.

And the more I thought about it, the more the swirling in my brain turned into the beginning of an idea. It was a big idea.

An idea like one of our Hard Reading Words: *audacious*: a willingness to take surprisingly bold risks.

I don't feel audacious, usually. But this idea was audacious. And maybe audacity was what it took to make friends.

I wondered if ideas were born the same way stars are, starting off small and collecting space clouds and dust until they have enough to burst open.

Silently I thanked Ms. Trepky for making Talia and me swap phone numbers and pulled my phone out of my backpack:

Hey, it's Libby from school. About Dustin—I have an idea. I think you'll like it.

SEND.

I lay back on my bed while I waited for her to respond, and I couldn't help grinning.

Being audacious was going to be fun.

The Doctor That Isn't Mine

A couple of days later Nonny had an appointment with the baby doctor.

And she said I could come.

When Mom picked me up after school, Nonny was in the passenger seat, waving at me while I ran to the car.

"How was school?" Mom asked.

"Great!" I said.

I didn't tell her about the plan Talia and I had made together. In the library. During lunch. Our scheme was set to take place early on Monday morning.

Talia liked my idea. I was glad she liked it. It meant that maybe, eventually, she'd like the person who'd come up with it. The person who was going to put the plan into action with her.

Me.

I slung my backpack into the seat next to me, and we drove to the doctor's office.

Not everyone feels this way, but doctors' offices make me feel safe. Maybe it's because I've spent so much time in them. I have the same doctors other people do, like a pediatrician and a dentist. Then I also have special doctors. I have a doctor who knows the most about Turner syndrome and my shots, called an endocrinologist. I have a doctor for my heart, called a cardiologist. And a doctor for my ears that don't hear so perfectly, called an ENT. That stands for ear, nose, and throat. Sometimes that makes me laugh. They didn't try super hard to come up with a creative name for that one, huh?

I like going to doctors even when it's someone new. Everything is clean and organized and you get to talk to someone who can fix things. Or who can make absolutely sure there's nothing broken. (My ear doctor even has a tiny camera hooked to a screen so when she pokes the camera stick in your ear your whole waxy eardrum pops up on the TV. It's pretty impressive!)

When we went back to the small white room,

Nonny lay down on the crinkly paper. It was actually a bit strange not being the one on the exam table. Nonny lifted her shirt, exposing her milk-skin belly that was recently beginning to pudge.

Dr. Willoughby rolled over on her stool and squeezed a glob of jelly onto Nonny's stomach, a blue, sparkly, toothpasty blob of stuff that might have been what genies are made of. Then Dr. Willoughby took what looked sort of like a white plastic showerhead and rubbed it into the blue goop and smeared it across Nonny's stomach.

And that's when something magic happened on the TV screen attached to the weird showerhead tool. (Doctors get the best TV!) The screen was nothing but gray fuzz, and then all of a sudden there was a black space in the fuzzy gray, and in that black space was a little bean.

A human bean.

Nonny's baby bean.

It looked like a space ship in the middle of a swirling, faraway galaxy.

Then there was a sound. A squishy, squelchy sound almost like stepping in mud, and it came like the ticking of a clock. *Squish. Squelch. Squooch.*

The bean had a heartbeat.

Dr. Willoughby smiled.

Nonny looked at Mom and smiled.

Mom put her hand over her mouth and made an *ohh* sound.

I couldn't stop looking at the tiny gray staticky bean. That was a baby on TV right there. Nonny's baby.

My baby.

Well, my niece. Or nephew. I was guessing niece.

Nonny's face made me think of one of our Hard Reading Words—*radiant*: glowing or emanating light.

Dr. Willoughby started talking to Nonny, explaining things, and even though I was only paying attention to the screen and the squelching noise, Dr. Willoughby's rolling-wave voice and sunshine eyes told me everything I needed to know.

While the adults talked about how big the tiny baby was, I stared at the screen. I looked at what Dr. Willoughby said was the baby's face. Little nose and lips. What if the baby was a little girl? What if she was born with moles on her cheeks like mine? What if she was short and had round ribs, too? And in the nanosecond space between squelches, one teeny, pinprick-size thought came poking through.

What if I wasn't alone?

Alone with missing chromosomes and a capital-*S* Syndrome?

No. No, that thought could go right back out of my head. It didn't make sense anyway. I wasn't alone. Not even close. I had two people right in this very room who knew every bit of me and loved me and stayed by me always. They were all I needed.

No, Nonny's baby was going to be tall and make friends the way her mom did. No needles, no surgeries. Nothing wrong, nothing missing.

See that, Cecilia? I said silently. *Can you hear that tiny, squishing heart? You won't let anything bad happen to that little protostar in Nonny's belly, will you? Our deal will work. It has to work.*

That tiny, squelching heart would keep on squelching for as long as I had anything to say about it.

Audacity

On Monday morning I woke up before my alarm.

Today was the day to be audacious.

I did my best not to fidget and rush too much. Even still, my mom said, "What's with you today, girly, you got ants in your pants?"

"I'm just in a hurry to get to school," I said.

I'd told Mom that I needed to get to school early that morning so I could work on a project with a friend. I think Mom was excited that I was doing something with a friend in the first place, so she didn't ask too many questions.

Technically what I told her wasn't a lie, but I still felt sort of guilty about it.

Before we loaded into the car, when Mom wasn't looking, I swiped the chocolate frosting from the pantry (the store-bought kind I eat with graham crackers, not my mom's good homemade stuff) and dropped the container into my backpack. Talia was bringing the other supplies.

When we pulled up to the school, I said a quick-as-a-rabbit goodbye to Mom and ran inside.

Talia was already there. Waiting for me by her locker.

By her left foot, she had a big green bucket full of sand and two little green shovels. And wonder of wonders, she grinned when she saw me. That made me grin, too.

"Ready?" she said.

I pulled the chocolate frosting out of my backpack. "Oh yes."

We'd picked early morning because we knew we'd be alone. The teachers were in meetings or in their classrooms. None of the other kids had come in yet. We were alone in the hallway, which was exactly what we needed to be.

We looked both ways, like we were crossing the street, and when we were absolutely positively certain nobody was there, we dashed to the smelly locker of Dustin Pierce. The big bucket of sand Talia was carrying didn't even slow her down because she was so strong. She could have arm-wrestled any-body in our class and she would have won. Maybe even Ms. Trepky, although I had a feeling Ms. Trepky was much stronger than she looked.

We both looked around again once we were at Dustin's locker. It really did smell like gym socks and old Doritos.

Talia looked at me for a moment, one eyebrow raised. Then she smiled again and handed me one of the green shovels. She scooped up a shovelful of sand, then slowly and carefully poured the sand through the slots in Dustin's locker.

A tiny stream of sand trickled through the crack in the bottom, but not much. Not so much you'd notice.

There was no turning back now.

I shoveled up another batch of sand and poured it through. I wasn't as neat about it as Talia was, and some fell out onto the floor. Talia glanced around, checking again that we were alone, and spread the fallen sand across the hall with her foot.

We scooped and scooped, looking at each other and glancing around the hall. Nobody came. I didn't hear a sound except for the shifting sand.

(Although Talia would have heard someone coming before I did anyway.) It was almost too easy.

When we'd poured as much sand as we could through the slots, Talia picked up the chocolate frosting. She popped open the lid.

"It's almost too good to waste on a turd like him," she said. Then she winked at me and dug out a big glob with her fingers.

PLOP! Straight onto the locker door went the frosting, leaving a mark of Talia's chocolaty handprint. She held the frosting tub out to me and I took my own big scoop.

PLOP! There was my hand, too.

Talia took another wad of frosting with her finger and started writing on the locker with the chocolate ink. She turned our handprints into two big piles of poop. She smeared more across the bottom of the locker and it stopped some of the sand from drizzling out. Then she wrote a big *BB*.

Take that, her face said.

I did my best to draw a small Frankenstein in the middle of my chocolate handprint, complete with scarred chin. It wasn't very good, but I thought the point got across.

Talia and I looked at our artwork. Then she

looked at her hand, then at me, and then raised her messy, chocolaty hand. I raised mine. We gave each other a splatting, goopy, chocolaty high five.

We grabbed our stuff and ran into the girls' bathroom down the hall, laughing like maniacs. Friend maniacs.

Friends and Consequences

There's a first time for everything, I guess.

Even a trip to the principal's office.

Talia and I sat on the other side of her desk, our hands between our knees. Principal Lopez looked at us, her bright red nails drumming on the desk.

"Girls," she said. "I know you two are smarter than this. Talia, I haven't known you very long but I know you are a smart girl. And Libby." She sighed. "I've known you since you were in kindergarten. This is not behavior I thought I'd see from you."

I kept staring at my knees. I couldn't look at her.

She was right. That was why I felt so bad. It was like something hadn't been working in my brain. Hadn't been connected. I hadn't thought one tiny little bit about what might happen after we poured the sand. Why hadn't I thought about that? Because I was only thinking about making Talia feel better. About making her happy.

About making her my friend.

And now here we were, waiting for our moms in Principal Lopez's office.

"Why didn't one of you come and tell me what had happened? With Dustin and the pictures," asked Ms. Lopez.

"How did you—" Talia said.

"Another student saw him do it," said Ms. Lopez. "You kids think you're so sneaky, but we know. So why didn't you tell us yourself?"

For a second nobody said anything. Then in a voice like a snapping turtle Talia said, "Like anyone would have cared."

I gulped, nervous that Talia was brave enough to talk like that to a grown-up. I thought Ms. Lopez might get angry, but when I glanced up at her face, she looked sad.

Ms. Lopez leaned forward over her desk, her arms out. "Talia, are you listening to me? I need you to listen." She put a hand flat down on her desk. "If anything has happened before, anything like this, and the adults you spoke with didn't believe you, or didn't take you seriously, then I want you to understand something. They were wrong. I want you to know that I will do my best to listen. I will always care."

Talia sat very still. Her ears were red.

"You should know," said Ms. Lopez, "that I have already spoken with Dustin and his mom, and heard his side of the story. I've got a letter of apology for you, Talia. He will be out of school for the next three days."

Then there was a knock on the door. When it opened, Mom walked in along with a woman who looked exactly like a grown-up Talia.

Mom had that nervous crease along her forehead. She mumbled, "Oh my goodness," and put a hand on my shoulder. Mrs. Latu said in a loud voice, "Now what's going on here?"

Principal Lopez explained what had happened. She explained about the big pile of sand in the hall that the janitor was cleaning up. I hadn't thought about the janitor having to clean up the sand. She explained about the chocolate frosting. She explained, too, about the pictures of butts in Talia's locker and how Dustin had already been sent home.

"Girl, girl, girl," said Mrs. Latu, shaking her

head. Her voice sounded stern, but her hand was softly patting Talia's thick, curly hair.

"Why didn't you tell me?" Mom whispered.

I didn't know what to say. Telling Mom that I'd kept quiet because Talia had told me to sounded too much like an excuse. Like I was blaming Talia. When really the sand was all my idea.

"Look," said Ms. Lopez. "It's been taken care of. I'm going to send you girls down the hall to help clean up, and then home for the day, okay? And when you come back I expect a letter of apology from each of you. Tomorrow you'll be back and ready to learn, yes? Without the sand?"

Talia and I nodded.

"And if anything like this happens again, please, please, come talk to me first. I am here to help you with exactly this kind of thing."

Mom promised that I would talk to her next time. Ms. Lopez stood and said goodbye, and we left her office.

We walked slowly down the hall, Talia and I keeping our eyes to the ground. Mom's hand stayed on my back, and it did make me feel a bit better. It helped me breathe easier. This wasn't a good thing, but it could have been worse. I could have been expelled. Or sent to prison.

"What does *BB* stand for anyway?" asked Mrs. Latu, as we neared the dreaded locker.

Talia glanced at me and we caught each other's eye. To my surprise, she was grinning.

"Beach bum," she said.

Some Dead White Dude

The next day, I was eating lunch in the library again, but this time it was different.

This time Talia was eating lunch with me.

We were lounging in the beanbag chairs by the magazine section. Talia's mom had sent her with a big Tupperware of rice with chicken and pineapple and a sweet sauce that smelled so good it made me shiver.

"Your mom seems like a really good cook," I said as I ate my peanut butter banana sandwich.

"Yeah," Talia said.

"My mom owns a bakery. We should do a combo dinner sometime."

I was scared that somehow that would be the

wrong thing to say, but Talia said, "My mom could do pork. Does your mom make coconut cream pie?"

"The best."

We both turned back to the open notebooks on our lap. I'd gotten better at remembering about Silent Questions, and earlier that day I'd figured out something new about Talia. We were both writers. At least kind of.

"How's it going?" I asked her.

She groaned. "I hate sonnets," she said.

Talia had signed up for the Creative Writing elective. She told me she was really excited about it at first, but that they were just doing boring stuff like essays and descriptive paragraphs. And sonnets.

"I keep trying to tell Mr. Gradey that rap counts. That Logic *is* poetry. But he won't listen."

I looked down at my notebook. I had a good chunk of my letter written, about how Cecilia had influenced the world, but I couldn't figure out how the letter should start. I wanted the first paragraph, even the first sentence, to be so wham-bam amazing that they would *have* to give it the grand prize.

"How's yours coming?" she asked.

"I thought I knew what to say, but it's harder than I thought," I said.

"What's yours for again?"

I cleared my throat. She'd liked my other plan, my sandy-locker plan, but I didn't know what she'd think about Cecilia Payne.

"It's for this contest at the Smithsonian. Ms. Trepky told us about it once, on the day you came. They're making a new Women in STEM exhibit, and you do a project to teach people about a woman scientist you think people should know about, and then you write a letter about it and submit it, and the winner gets twenty-five thousand dollars."

Talia choked on the piece of chicken she was eating. "Twenty-five thousand dollars?"

"I know."

"Dude. You've gotta win this."

"I know. Then I could use the money to help my sister when her husband is looking for a better job."

I said it without thinking, and then right away wondered if this was one of those wrong things to say. One of those times when what I thought or said was strange or weird, and I didn't know it until afterward, when people gave me funny looks.

I'd keep the Universe Deal to myself, but now Talia knew why I wanted that money, and I had no idea if she'd think I was being naive or dumb or silly.

But she didn't. She nodded, looking thoughtful and focused, if I was reading her face right. "Who are you writing about?" she asked.

"Mine's about . . . well, there's this woman—her name is Cecilia—and she was a professor at Harvard a long time ago and she figured out what stars are made of. Like the chemicals and stuff. Then another professor sort of took credit. It's a little complicated. But anyway, she's not in our textbook. And I think she should be."

Talia leaned back in her beanbag. "She figured out all that about stars, and she's not in our textbook? That's dumb."

"Exactly!" I said.

She looked up at the ceiling for a minute, her long dark hair billowing around her face like a cloud of thought.

"Start simple," she said. "Say, 'Listen, I may be a young girl, but I'm writing to you about something very important.'"

I paused, my pencil held above the paper. "Hey, that's really good." I scribbled the words down before they left my brain. I'd type everything out nice and neat later.

She sighed again. "And yet I can't come up with a freaking thing to say about . . . what did he call it? 'Petrarchan love.' I don't know what to say about some dead white dude."

"Hey," I said. "That's what your sonnet should be called."

"What?"

"'Some Dead White Dude.'"

Talia laughed so hard she snorted. "Oh man, Mr. Gradey won't like that very much. I'll do it."

She crossed out a few lines she'd written and wrote *"Some Dead White Dude"* in big letters. I hoped I wasn't getting her in trouble again. My dad says it's important to be a Good Influence Friend, and I couldn't tell if I was being one or not.

But by the end of lunch, she had her poem written.

And by the end of lunch, I had my letter.

How Grown-Ups Listen

I had waited what felt like days and days after sending the email to Knight-Rowell Publishing, and still hadn't heard anything. That's when I decided to call.

A woman with a high-pitched voice answered. "Knight-Rowell Publishing. How may I assist you?"

I cleared my throat. I had my answer ready.

"Hello. May I please speak with Trent Hickman?"

That was the name on the title page of my textbook. Right next to *Edited by*.

"I'm afraid Mr. Hickman isn't available for phone calls, but I would be happy to take a message for you."

I imagined this woman in too-high heels that made it hard to walk and hair pulled so far back you could see up her nose.

"Well, I really need to speak with him," I said. "When would he be available?"

"I can take a message for you and he will get back to you as soon as possible. What was your name?"

Her voice sounded even higher.

Maybe he had his own separate email, and my note from the form on the website hadn't gotten to him. "What about his email?" I said.

"I'm afraid I can't give out that information, but if you'll tell me your name I'll pass along the message."

I fell back onto my bed. "Libby Monroe." I told the woman I needed to speak with him as soon as possible, and I gave her my phone number.

"And what is this about?" she asked.

"It's about Cecilia Payne," I said.

I waited for her to say something else, to say goodbye and hang up, but she paused for a second and then asked, "How old are you?"

I was 98 percent sure this was not a woman who took twelve-year-olds seriously.

"Please have him call me," I said.

Then we hung up.

I was 98 percent sure he would never get my message.

I looked at my poster of the Milky Way. If he never called it only meant I'd have to try something else. A star didn't stop burning just because some space debris got in its way. Maybe an actual mailed letter would work. After a bit of looking around on the website, I found the Knight-Rowell Publishing address. I got to work writing another letter, a letter especially to Mr. Trent Hickman about a certain smart woman scientist who I thought should be in his textbook.

Second Draft

I printed and carefully folded my letter to Mr. Trent Hickman, and put it in the mailbox, sending my words and wishes out into the world. And the words didn't stop there, either. I also gave Ms. Trepky my Smithsonian Cecilia Payne letter to look at.

Look how much progress we're making, I told Cecilia. *Ms. Trepky is going to help me help you.*

The very next day, Ms. Trepky was waiting for me by the door after class. She had a manila envelope in her hand. "Libby, may I see you for one moment?" she said.

I slid my book into my backpack and zipped up slowly, waiting for everyone else to leave. When I laid my letter down on Ms. Trepky's desk the day before, I hadn't been nervous. But now she was holding the words I'd written, worked so carefully on, ready to tell me all the things that were wrong with them. Worth it, of course, because this had to be the greatest writing ever, but still. Walking toward her and her feedback felt a little like walking into surgery.

Ms. Trepky set the envelope in my hands. "First," she said, "I wanted to tell you that you did a fantastic job. Your enthusiasm is infectious and makes reading about Cecilia a joy. Your explanations are clear and your descriptions evocative."

"Really?" I said.

"Absolutely," she said. "I want you to remember that when you open this envelope. I didn't hold back, Libby. I know you're taking this seriously, and my feedback reflects that. I wrote up a short edit letter that you'll find stapled to the front, and then I made in-line notations as well. Don't be overwhelmed when you see the red marks. Every professional writer gets these edit letters and red marks to make their work sparkle. This truly is an excellent first draft, and I look forward to reading the project portion of the letter as you complete it."

I looked at the envelope, half expecting it to start bleeding red ink. If Ms. Trepky thought I could handle this like a professional, I would. My last two classes of the day were going to be stare-at-the-clock classes while I waited to get home and get to work.

"Thank you," I said. "Thank you so, so much."

"My privilege," said Ms. Trepky. She sounded like she meant it.

When I finally got home I didn't pause for a snack but went straight to my room and opened up the manila envelope. I flipped past the edit letter and saw the red marks like a very bad case of the chicken pox.

Step by step. I'd just have to take it step by step. First thing was the edit letter, talking about big things like smoother transitions in certain parts, or suggestions for the next part of the letter, getting specific about how Cecilia inspired me, a girl with Turner syndrome.

So much to do. So much shifting and rearranging before I even got to the red pox. I kept at it, slicing and dicing, cleaning and polishing.

Red started swirling behind my eyes and I knew I needed a break. Time for that missed snack.

On the way back to my room, a cup of grapes in one hand, I stopped in front of Nonny's room. She was talking to someone.

"... isn't under your jurisdiction, though. You shouldn't have to cover for people so much."

I had to scoot close to the door to hear. It sounded like she was on the phone with Thomas.

"I know," she said. "Yeah, I . . . that's . . . I hate the way they're treating you. I know, but I wish there was something else . . . I hate this."

I put my hand on the wall.

"I wish you were here," she said.

My cup of grapes and I went back to my room. I sat on my bed, staring at those red marks.

If swimming through that red ink could get Nonny her wish, I'd dog-paddle my way across the Pacific Ocean.

Houston, We
Have a Problem

The air outside got colder and colder, and I still had zero response from Knight-Rowell Publishing. No response to my emails, or my letter. That's when Nonny's nausea started getting worse. I texted Talia about it and she said that her mom got sick a lot when she was pregnant with her little brother and sister, and that it was pretty normal. To me, though, this didn't seem like Normal Pregnant Sick. This seemed Very Not Normal.

I paced nervously from my bedroom to the living room, hearing Nonny vomit and dry heave in the bathroom. Every time I saw Nonny's gray face and heard those gasping, retching sounds, I thought, *This is what failure looks like. This is what it sounds like, hints at what could happen if I don't get this right.*

Nonny barely had the energy to stand up. She hadn't kept anything down in almost thirty-two hours. I was keeping track.

Are you trying to warn me, Cecilia? I thought. *I know all the things that can go wrong. I won't let them. I will work harder and harder. As hard as it takes.*

This was way bigger than tea and marmalade.

I found Mom in the kitchen kneading dough with a Grand Canyon furrow between her brows, barely even noticing what her hands were doing. The dough looked pulverized. It looked like I felt.

"Mom, what can we do?" I said.

She looked at me for a few moments, then picked up her phone. Half an hour later we were at the hospital. Mom, Dad, and me, waiting with brow creases and fidgety feet in a too-small room while nurses put an IV in Nonny's arm.

The attendants kept saying, "She just needs fluids, she'll be okay." And I believed them, like I normally do, but it was the first time I didn't like being around doctors and nurses. In fact, I hated it, because it meant my sister was less safe than if she'd been able to drink a normal glass of water in the first place.

After a few hours with fluids, Nonny looked

more relaxed. Less shaky. But she looked exhausted, with dark purple circles under her eyes. Even though she did look a little better and was breathing more normally, I knew I never wanted to see her like this again. I would rather be the one in the hospital bed myself. A million times rather.

And even though I trusted, this time, that she would get better, somehow it still felt like seeing a glimpse of what the future would be like if I failed in my deal with Cecilia Payne. What if I didn't win the grand prize and couldn't calm Nonny's financial black hole? And what if Thomas never found a good job and I couldn't help them?

And what if the baby had something that could *never* get better? Something that maybe meant a damaged heart or kidney and shots every day? What if she was scared of shots like Thomas? What if there was someone in the baby's class who thought they were super clever about mean nicknames? Or worse?

This was why it didn't matter if I was the only one with Turner syndrome—because the alternative was a whole lot worse. Maybe even dangerous.

And there was another thing. A silly thing, maybe. Because really, no matter what, Mom and

Nonny would look at me the way they always had. The way that said, *You are my sister who I love no matter what*, and, *You are my daughter who I love with my whole universe no matter what*. They'd look at the new baby the same way, too, no matter what. But in the place inside your head, the only person you've got there looking at you and talking to you is yourself. Like you're staring into a mirror that shows what you really look like on the inside, and if I failed in this deal, even if nobody else knew, I'd know. It'd be like a sticky note taped to the corner of my Inside Mirror that said, *Here's another thing you missed.*

Here's another thing you couldn't do.

I'd recently watched a documentary on the History Channel about the Apollo space missions and how dangerous and important they were. The title of the show came into my head while I sat in that hospital room.

Failure Is Not an Option.

What's in a Name?

Nonny came home pretty quickly, with the assignment to get lots of rest. The doctors said morning sickness like this was a bit unusual, but that she'd be okay if she drank lots and didn't overdo it. Mostly things went back to normal, but any time Nonny only nibbled her food, Mom's face seemed to get one more tiny wrinkle. Other times I'd hear Nonny on the phone with Thomas, worrying about what they were going to do for his next job, telling him how much she missed him. Those times were reminders for me. Reminders of how important my mission was.

Her baby bump was also starting to show. That

was another reminder. She wasn't nearly at bowling-ball level yet, but there was a roundness in her belly that you could tell was something special.

I sent another email through the Knight-Rowell Publishing website. And I wrote another letter to Mr. Trent Hickman.

Nonny had this look that I started to think of as the After the Doctor Look. Usually her appointments were during school, so I didn't get to go after the first one, but when I walked in the door and she was on the couch with the sugar-glazed eyes and more light in the room came from her face than from the lamp by the piano, I knew she'd seen one of those TV-static pictures of her baby.

One day when I came in from school, before I could even drop my backpack in my room, she grinned at me wide and patted the seat next to her. "Come here, I want to tell you something."

I slid my bag onto the floor and hopped onto the couch next to her. I wanted to snuggle up to her, but I didn't because I also wanted to look at her face and the swirl of fireworks happening in her eyes.

"We went to the doctor today. We've sort of

known the gender for a while but today it was definitely confirmed. And . . . and I talked to Thomas and we've picked out a name."

I bounced up and down. "You did? Boy or girl? It's a girl, isn't it? What's the name?"

"Yes, it's a girl. She's a little girl."

More bouncing. "You're having a girl! I'm going to have a niece!"

"And we've decided to name her Cecilia."

I stopped bouncing.

I felt a jolt between my shoulders.

"Are you okay?" Nonny said. "Do you not like the name?"

"I . . ." I swallowed, gripping the edge of the gray couch cushion. I wished I could get such a grip on my own thoughts. If I'd had any doubts about my deal with the universe—with Cecilia—I couldn't doubt anymore.

This was like Cecilia herself calling me up on the phone.

I hear you, I thought.

"I like it," I finally managed to say. "I love it. What . . . what made you choose it?"

"Well, it's Thomas's grandmother's name," she said. "And I think it's beautiful."

"It *is* beautiful," I said. I looked at Nonny, at the tiny girl growing in her belly, and then looked out to the sky. I made a promise to all three. "And your baby will be beautiful. She will be perfect."

Textbook People's People

More and more time went by without any word from Mr. Trent Hickman at Knight-Rowell Publishing. Calling on the phone wasn't helping, either.

I needed a new plan.

A phase two.

Pacing helped the juices flow and I began walking between my bed and my desk, back and forth, over and over.

I only had a short amount of time left. Just a few months until the baby was due. If I was going to keep my deal with Cecilia Payne, PhD, I was going to have to start thinking big.

I even thought about flying to New York. I thought about marching up the steps into the office of Knight-Rowell Publishing and standing firm until Trent Hickman *had* to see me. Except where would I get the money for a ticket? How would I convince my parents to let me go? I'd told them I was working on a special project but hadn't told them too much about it yet because when I won twenty-five thousand freaking dollars, I wanted it to be a super-amazing eye-buggingly spectacular surprise. Besides, if I talked too much about it then I might have to go into the whole Universe Deal thing, and at least for right now, that needed to stay in a warm, secret place inside me.

For the first time since I'd come up with my project plan, I heard one tiny, buzzy voice in the back corner of my brain wondering if I was too small for a plan so big. Nothing could ever make me give up, of course. But if we didn't even learn about Cecilia Payne in school, the person who had discovered these amazing things about the universe, how hard was a new audacious plan going to be for a scar-hearted girl eating yogurt while her mom braided her hair?

Then I had Ms. Trepky's class.

"How many of you have heard of Rosa Parks?" she started. Most of us raised our hands. (We'd read about her in our assigned reading, so it wasn't smart that Dustin didn't raise his hand because then Ms. Trepky knew he hadn't done his home-work.)

We talked about Rosa Parks for a while. We talked about how she was brave. Ms. Trepky wrote the words *Civil Disobedience* on the whiteboard and we talked about following the leaders of our world, and thinking for ourselves, and the times those two things overlap, and the times they don't.

"Now," said Ms. Trepky. "How many of you have heard of Claudette Colvin?"

At first I was worried, because I hadn't heard of her, and I thought maybe I'd missed something in our reading, but when I looked around, nobody else was raising their hand, either.

"Claudette Colvin did what Rosa Parks did. She refused to move to the back of the bus when some-one told her to, and she got arrested. Plus, she did it nine months before Rosa Parks."

So Ms. Trepky knew about people who should have been in our textbook, too. How many were there? A hundred? A thousand?

I raised my hand.

"So why isn't she in our textbook?"

Ms. Trepky looked at us, scanning our faces.

"That's a very good question," she said. "It's hard to say why certain people gain renown and others do not. Perhaps another way to think about it is this: If we had a textbook with everyone of importance, we would need a textbook with everyone."

She let us think about that for a minute. I pictured myself in a textbook, my face a small square photo next to a block of text and a heading with my name. I imagined a girl just like me reading about . . . me. What would it say? I looked around and imagined a section about everyone in the class. Even Dustin would have a section. That made me want to laugh.

Maybe I didn't need a section in a history textbook, but I still thought I knew someone who did.

Don't worry, Cecilia. I've got this.

"The point is," Ms. Trepky continued, "both of these women had an influence, even though we tend to study only one of them. And there are many, many more whose names we do not know. People who sat at counters and didn't leave, people who carried signs, people who got sprayed down with fire hoses. Each of them played a part in changing laws and shaping our country, and even though we've read a lot about people like Rosa Parks and Martin Luther King and Malcolm X, it wasn't just these few people who changed things. They needed help. Think of Martin Luther King's friends and parents and family who helped him. He was a Martin Luther King *junior*, after all, with a father who bequeathed him his own name. We would likely not even have him in our textbook if it wasn't for them."

Ms. Trepky sat on the edge of her desk. I could have sworn she was looking at me when she said, "One individual can make an incredible difference, but that individual is shaped and created and influenced by thousands of other people. And that person shapes and creates and influences thousands of other individuals in return."

I felt Ms. Trepky's words slide under my skin and into my bones. The words had so much truth it felt like a rainstorm on my head. I knew exactly what she meant. The world was shaped by billions and billions of unknown hands, by people living their own lives and thinking their own ideas across the whole planet, changing the universe just by being there. That meant I could sculpt and write on the DNA of the universe from my little corner of it, too, no matter my smallness or genetics or scars. I saw my own constellation spinning around in my head, the constellation that made me, the constellation of my family and bakeries and libraries and Nonny and a bright new Ms. Trepky star. Together, it was the universe that had reached out and shaped me like a clay sculpture, missing bits and scarred bits and all.

Now it was time for me to put my hands out into the universe and shape it back.

Twitterpated

I talked to Talia about it after school. "I really have to do something. Cecilia is depending on me."

I said it, even though she didn't know there were two Cecilias depending on me now.

Talia and I sat down on the sidewalk, leaning against the school while we waited for our parents. "I mean, my cousin is a flight attendant," she said. "I could ask her about flights to New York or something."

"I don't know. I need to think."

"Hmm."

We sat quietly, and Talia started tapping her thumb against the concrete. She had this weird, funky rhythm she would tap out whenever she was thinking.

"Hey, how did that poem go?" I said. "The dead white dude one?"

Talia stopped tapping. "It went . . . okay, actually. I think."

"Yeah?"

"Yeah. Mr. Gradey gave me another sonnet to read, but this time it was Shakespeare, and it was . . . good."

"He read your poem and then gave you *more* sonnets?"

"Yeah, because Shakespeare was sort of making fun of sonnets, too. At least in this one. It's about how . . . well, it starts, *My mistress' eyes are nothing like the sun.*"

"*Not* like the sun?"

"Yeah, weird, huh? He even talks about her stinky breath."

"Seriously? In a love sonnet?"

"Yeah. I know. But it's still a love sonnet."

I saw our blue van pull up, and Mom waved to me. I scooped up my backpack.

"I have an idea," Talia said. "Have you checked his Twitter?"

"Twitter?"

"Yeah, the editor guy. I bet he has a Twitter account."

I slapped my hand on my forehead. "Oh duh! How could I not think of that?"

Sometimes when my mind spun circles around one bright idea—when I got into tunnel vision mode—I had a hard time seeing the other options and strategies, like they were hiding in the shadows, away from the glare of the sun.

"I'll check it right when we get home," I said, running to the car.

"Update me tomorrow," Talia said.

As soon as we got home I said a mega-fast hello to Nonny (who was lying down on the couch— she'd been doing that a lot the last little while) and bolted to the computer in my room.

Mr. Trent Hickman *did* have a Twitter account. Of course he did.

I spent about ten minutes scrolling through his Twitter page. He tweeted about submissions, about his cat, and there were also a remarkable number of quotes from some writer called Ayn Rand. At first I felt excited scrolling through his tweets, like looking down the key of a treasure map. Then after more about cats and more about Ayn Rand, I started losing momentum. What was I expecting, anyway? What exactly was it that I was looking for?

Then I saw it.

A tweet from last September:

New conf schedule up on website. Come see me if you're in NY, FL, TX, or CO!

CO. I'd never been so excited to see those two letters in my entire life.

I clicked so fast on the link that I nearly dropped the mouse. It led me to the calendar page of Mr. Hickman's personal website.

The Texas and Florida events were past. So were a couple in New York, but he still had another one at NYU at the end of the year.

And he was coming to the University of Colorado in Boulder. In January.

It was too perfect. Nonny's baby name, now this.

I about kicked myself in the head for not seeing this before. For not thinking about checking it out earlier. But it wasn't too late.

All of this was meant to happen. I could do this one thing for Cecilia Payne, and she'd be the centerpiece of this deal that would make a happy home for Nonny and Thomas, a perfect, healthy baby. This was my sculpture, the universe I was molding for my sister and her little family. What could be more important—what was I here in my universe to make but this?

Out Loud

I couldn't quite wrap my brain around the fact that Mr. Trent Hickman, editor at Knight-Rowell Publishing, was coming to Boulder. This was my chance to meet him, to get going on this project for my Smithsonian essay. But I couldn't figure out what to do about it. I kept seeing Nonny's face when she was sick in the hospital, and it made it even harder to think and plan because I had to get this right. It was like I'd been chugging along and suddenly the wheel had come off the track. My brain did that to me sometimes, when my bright tunnel vision plan needed to be changed or adjusted.

So I knew I needed to talk it through with someone.

I didn't get a chance to talk to Talia before school started, but I hurried to her locker as soon as the lunch bell rang.

"Talia!"

She slammed her locker and when she looked at me her cheeks were pink. At first I was scared I'd done something wrong and she was mad at me, but when she saw me she sighed and smiled and said, "Hey, Libby."

"Are you okay?" I asked.

She sighed again and gave her lunch bag a swing. "Yeah, I'm fine."

I opened my mouth to ask her something else, but right then I remembered the Silent Questions. This was a perfect moment for them. In my brain I asked her every question I had. In my imagination I knew exactly what to say and do to make Talia feel better.

Nonny was right, of course.

After a couple of seconds, Talia started talking again.

"It's . . . well, Mr. Gradey keeps bugging me about this Poetry Out Loud contest thing."

Now it was time for an out-loud question. "What's that?" I asked.

"Oh, you submit a poem and perform it at this

contest and the winners go on to the next round and all that crap."

"But . . . you'd be great at that! You'd be amazing!"

Talia huffed. "I probably wouldn't win. I don't know. I mean, nobody would care."

"Would *you* care? About doing the contest, I mean?"

Talia shrugged, but her eyes weren't shrugging. Her eyes were swirling.

"Isn't this sort of what you like? You said you want to be a rap artist, right? Well this is sort of maybe—"

"Who's ever heard of a Samoan rapper. I mean, there aren't even hardly any girl rappers. Plus you can't make a living as a musician anyway."

I couldn't think of the right question to ask, or the right thing to say, so I practiced another Silent Question.

Then she said, "Nobody cares what I say anyway."

The Silent Question had worked again.

"I think they would," I said. "If they heard you say it."

Talia gave her lunch bag another swing. "Anyway, so what did you find out?"

"Oh yeah!" I nearly popped out of my boots. "It's

so perfect it's almost freaky. He's coming to Boulder! To UC!"

"Who?"

"Trent Hickman. The editor. He's coming here!"

"No way. Seriously?"

"I know!"

We started walking toward the library.

"So when's he coming?" Talia asked.

"January twenty-sixth."

We took a few more steps, both quiet and thoughtful. Then she glanced at me and gave me that mischievous beach bum smile.

"That gives us about two months," she said, "to formulate a plan."

Thanksgiving Break

Thanksgiving turned out to be smaller than usual. Sometimes we had friends and extended family over, and sometimes the people who worked with Mom at the bakery, but this year it was only Mom, Dad, Nonny, and me. Plus of course on-the-way-baby Cecilia, if you counted her, which I did.

And we missed Thomas. He had to stay in Florida because of the extra holiday pay. If I could get this plan to work, maybe it would be enough to get them started so he'd never have to do something like that again. I sent him a Marco Polo of the table with all the food. When he responded he said, "Save that whole turkey leg for me, okay, Lobster?"

Sitting around the table was the first time I

noticed how much Nonny's baby bump was beginning to show. It was full-on cantaloupe size now, and bumped the table when she sat down.

"Incoming!" she said, and we laughed.

We talked about the baby a lot. I liked talking about her. But sometimes there was this thing that happened. Sometimes Nonny would get this sort of dazed smile and she would say something new her pregnant body was doing—her back was starting to ache, she was feeling too hot most of the time—and then Mom would join in and talk about when she was pregnant with Nonny or me and how she could tell differences, like how I was so much more wiggly, and Mom and Nonny would both talk and talk. Then after a moment one of them would glance over at me, and if I caught the look in time it was like they were remembering that I wouldn't ever have kids like that, wouldn't ever feel what they were feeling. And when they looked at me like that, I remembered, too.

Nonny also told us how Thomas was doing, how hard his job was. How he asked about their baby every day.

Dad and Thomas wouldn't ever get pregnant, either, I thought. I mean, that wasn't quite the same thing, but when I imagined Dad with a big, stretched belly, it made me laugh.

The dinner of yams and turkey and stuffing was delicious of course, but the real best part of my family's Thanksgiving is the pies. I mean, that's just how it works when your mom owns a bakery. She's a little bit insane, and every year she makes an entire pie for each one of us. The whole house smells sugary and the kitchen counters are smooth with grease.

Here's what she makes:

1. Pecan for Dad. Sturdy, filling, and a bit nutty.
2. Very berry for herself. Sweet, lively, and with plenty of cream on top.
3. A light, delicate, smooth, and perfect lemon meringue for Nonny.
4. All-American apple pie for Thomas. (She made it even though Thomas wasn't there. We sent a Marco Polo of all of us taking a bite.)
5. And a time-honored, sweet-but-savory, faithful pumpkin pie for me.

Nobody ever wants to share theirs, but it's epic how much pie we go through in one sitting.

I'd texted Talia over the break, working on our plan for the day Mr. Trent Hickman came to town. I wanted to text her and invite her over for one day during Thanksgiving break, but this voice in my head kept saying, *What if she doesn't want to come over?* Then that night, while we were watching *Babe* and trying to digest all that pie, she texted me again:

Talia: *I've got news, and it's good and bad. Guess what day Poetry Out Loud is.*

Me: *Don't tell me. Jan 26.*

Talia: *Yup. :) :(??*

I leaned back against the couch and tried to focus on the movie. Changing plans didn't work so well in my brain, and not having Talia with me for the master plan was not a good change. Sometimes, though, when I forgot about the plans for a second and thought about something else, then when I came back to the plan, everything fit a little better in my brain again.

If nothing stops me, even this, I thought, *then you'll make sure nothing hurts Nonny or her baby, right, Cecilia? You'll help me bring Thomas home?*

About ten minutes later I texted Talia back:

Me: *You go win that. You've got to. And I'll go win this. And thus ends step one in our master plan to rule the world!*

Silence

In Ms. Trepky's homeroom, sometimes we have silent reading time. It's actually pretty quiet compared to other classes when we're meant to be having silent preparation time of some kind, because Ms. Trepky's good at that, but there's still the occasional rustle and whisper that goes on.

Ms. Trepky was at her desk doing her own reading, and Talia was out for a bathroom break. I thought I heard something going on behind me, but I tried to focus on my Eleanor Roosevelt book.

The rustle behind me kept happening, but I couldn't make out what it was until finally I heard my name. I turned around. Angie and Patreece were sitting behind me, and when I looked back at them, they laughed.

"We've been saying your name for, like, five minutes," Angie said. "Couldn't you hear us?"

"Are you, like, deaf or something?" Patreece said.

"Ladies," said Ms. Trepky.

Angie and Patreece snickered one more time, then looked down at their books. I realized that they weren't saying my name in a get-my-attention way. They were saying it in a teasing way.

I went back to reading. I had my own work to think about. *Cecilia? And . . . Eleanor, too, if you're there? I'm gonna keep reading and focusing on you guys, because what those girls are whispering definitely doesn't matter, right?*

I was glad when the bell rang.

I took my lunch to the library, like usual. Talia had been spending quite a few lunch periods with Mr. Gradey and the drama teacher working on her Poetry Out Loud piece. I thought it was fantastic that she was entering, and that she was already working so hard. I knew she was going to win. But even though I tried not to, I couldn't help thinking that the library wasn't quite as good a best friend as it was before. It was still pretty great, of course, but it wasn't quite as good at telling jokes and showing me new rap songs and helping me with my master plan.

I ate my lunch and wrote down some ideas in my notebook. Talia had mentioned that her grandma in Samoa wasn't doing so well, and I knew she was worried about that, too. I didn't quite know how to tell her I missed her, not when she was so busy, and so sad about her grandma. I didn't quite know how to say that when she was ready, when she wanted to talk about her grandma and be worried, or when she'd won her contest and wanted to be excited, I'd be in the library.

Sound

Sometimes it's snow that signals the beginning of the Christmas season. Sometimes it's decorations, or special chocolates in the stores.

For me, when we get Mom's old record player and box of Christmas records out from the attic, *that's* when I know Christmas is coming.

It's when John Denver and Rowlf the dog start singing about having a "merry little Christmas." That's when I know it's really happening.

It's when Mom and Nonny sit at the piano and play along with the records and I watch from the couch and we sing along, especially, this year, to "Grandma Got Run Over by a Reindeer" because next time around Mom really will be a grandma and that is totally crazy.

But this year, a small but dark buzz of worry glommed onto the back of my brain, like one little seagull trying to snatch your sandwich on an otherwise blue-sky, pristine day at the beach. Like the clock Cinderella must have heard ticking down the minutes toward midnight at the best night she'd ever had. That same clock must have been tick-ticking in my head.

Because on these days we played good music and ate delicious food, and everyone was laughing and happy. There were songs coming from the record player and the piano and I wanted to listen, without any distraction, but underneath that music a worry kept counting down in my head. A baby was coming. The baby of my perfect, wonderful sister, so of course the baby would be perfect and wonderful, too, and probably also really good at piano. And maybe Mom and Nonny and the new baby would all play piano together, because of course the baby will learn how to play the piano very easily and very early. I bet she could even be a prodigy. But if I sort of can't play the piano so great, how can I be the Best Aunt Ever to a piano prodigy?

Plus there's something that might even be worse.

Because what if it's the opposite? What if I fail

my deal and she *is* born with something wrong?
Wrong with her heart or her brain?

What if she is born with a missing piece?

A missing chromosome?

Would it be my fault?

Eleanor Roosevelt

We did our Historical Figure presentations the week before Christmas break. I'd been spending my lunches working by myself on my letter to give to Mr. Trent Hickman when he came to Boulder, but of course I hadn't forgotten my presentation.

Talia went first, and read a wonderful poem she'd written about Langston Hughes, and taught us some of his style and about the Harlem Renaissance. I knew she'd wanted to do someone from Samoa, but there weren't any in our textbook. More people missing, I guess. I told her she could find a world-changing Samoan for next semester's presentation, and I thought it was pretty smart of Ms. Trepky to make us look outside the textbook for people to study.

Then Dustin played a video he'd made about Buffalo Bill, and even though it was silly and goofy and went on too long, he remembered to teach us actual things about Mr. Bill, like how he fought for the Union in the Civil War.

And I did my presentation on Eleanor Roosevelt. I used a PowerPoint, because PowerPoints make me more comfortable.

When I pulled up the first picture of Eleanor Roosevelt, though, Dustin and his cronies snickered from the back row.

"Something's wrong with that lady's chin," Dustin said. "Is that why you picked her?" More snickers.

Then I had something that maybe could be called a Silent Moment. I don't mean I suddenly went deaf. What I mean is that it felt like I could see everybody in the room as if they were moving in slow motion, slow enough for me to read their faces. I saw Dustin look back and forth at his two buddies and I knew he was saying whatever he thought might make them laugh, might make them think he was cool. Ms. Trepky was standing in the back of the room, and I saw her look down at Dustin, ready to stop the nonsense. Except then she looked at me and I knew she was asking me a

Silent Question, asking me if I wanted to respond to the Nonsense Boys myself.

I did.

"Well," I said. "Since you're kind enough to bring that up, I'll start with a quote from Ms. Eleanor Roosevelt, who, if you'll remember, was First Lady of the United States." I clicked ahead in my PowerPoint to a page with a big block quote. "She said, 'No one can make you feel inferior without your consent.' And so I think, since we're trying to figure out these historical figures like they were our best friends, what I think is that if Eleanor were here right now, she wouldn't care at all what you thought of her chin. And not like she was trying to ignore it and she secretly *did* care. No, what I think is that if she heard you say that, she might look at you and smile and maybe even blow you a kiss with that weird mouth and then go back to talking to people who had more interesting things to say."

Dustin's face was red, and his shoulders slumped. I did feel a tiny bit bad for being mean like that. Only a tiny bit, though, because saying those things out loud made me realize something. It made me realize that sometimes I only *pretended* not to care when people whispered my name and I couldn't hear, or about my neck being thick on the sides, or being one of the slowest runners in PE. I wanted to know how to *really* not care. How to spend more time thinking about more important things. Like Eleanor.

Ms. Trepky was smiling.

I finished my presentation on Eleanor Roosevelt.

I got an A.

Gray Walls and Gas Masks

Here's something I learned: Sometimes what a place looks like on the outside changes depending on how you feel on the inside.

To explain what I'm talking about, let me tell you about the Denver International Airport.

Some airports are big, and some are small. Some are square and glass, some are brown and flat. Some, like the Denver airport, look like a long spiky row of white circus tents.

There are quite a few unique things about the Denver airport. I looked it up once.

The Denver airport is the biggest airport in the country, by almost two times, and is the third largest in the world.

There's a blue stallion statue near the entrance

that has sort of devilish eyes and it fell over and killed its sculptor while it was being made. There are also psychedelic murals throughout the airport, many showing crowds of people with strange faces and rainbow-colored clothes jammed in with jaguars and tropical flowers. On one, there's a Nazi soldier in a wrinkly, pale gas mask, next to a letter from a little boy who died at Auschwitz. I don't know why a painter would want to paint that. Or why airport staff would want to hang it on the wall.

The Denver airport is a weird airport.

Sometimes you're in a strange gray place with even stranger paintings and statues and it feels like you're in a horror movie and the painted people are watching you.

And then someone you love comes, like maybe your sister's husband who the whole family is there at the airport to pick up, who your sister hasn't seen in months. And then it's him in his jeans and T-shirt and your sister's arms wrapped around his neck being reflected in the shiny chrome walls, and in the reflection you see him bend down and give her pregnant belly a big kiss, and the rainbow-clothed people look happy, too, and even when you remember the horse statue out front it doesn't seem so demonic, just a little mischievous.

It cost two billion dollars *more* than they expected to build the Denver airport. I think it was worth it.

Long Distance

A short while after our Historical Figure presentations, Talia left. Another person at the Denver airport, going instead of coming. Her grandma in Samoa was getting worse. Maybe even dying. So her whole family was spending a few weeks there. They were spending Christmas there. She wouldn't be back until January.

It made me feel stupid for not inviting her over during Thanksgiving break. Or on a weekend. Why hadn't I invited her over already? Now I wouldn't be able to for the rest of the month.

Now I would be working on my plan alone.

Having Thomas home made everyone happy. He and Nonny stayed next to each other all the time, holding hands, talking, eating. Trying not to worry too much about work and money, from what I could tell.

Nonny said she was trying to enjoy the time they had before he had to leave again.

She said she hated long distance.

Doctor Who Was Right

Dad and I are staunch buddies, that is absolutely true, but there are a lot of ways we are very different. Dad likes to go on runs in the cold, early morning before he goes to school, and to me that sounds like the absolute worst thing ever. I can barely make a lap around the gym in PE. Dad's hands are always moving, sketching, fiddling, and in his classroom he has some absolutely amazing paintings that look like Monet could have done them. Me? Nothing I draw or paint turns out looking like I intended it to. I can manage to mess up stick figures.

There's one special thing that Dad and I have in common, though. One show we look forward to watching together, just him and me.

Doctor Who.

It's sort of a tradition for me and Dad that we watch every Christmas special in the series on Christmas Eve.

Mom and Nonny put up with it.

In one of my favorite episodes, the Doctor is talking about how life isn't simply good or bad, but a pile of good things and a pile of bad things. And the good things maybe don't solve the bad things, but the bad things don't make the good things unimportant.

I think about that a lot.

Here are my Christmas Piles.

Good Pile: Mom and Dad holding hands on the couch, barely able to keep their eyes open because they're so tired. Thomas tugging Nonny under the mistletoe every chance he gets. Homemade snickerdoodles. Rolos in my stocking. A book about Rosalind Franklin, the woman who helped discover what DNA looks like (my parents know me pretty well). Baby Cecilia somehow knowing it was Christmas, too, and dancing around so fierce in Nonny's tummy we all got to put our hands on her belly and feel the baby kick. When I felt it for the first time I said, "Hello, Cecilia, welcome to the family!" Then Nonny's smile when she opened the music box I ordered online. When you opened the lid a miniature solar system emerged and began orbiting. And it played a Celtic Woman song.

Here's the Bad Pile: I bought Mom a candle and a pretty cookbook, and she said she loved it, and it's not that I don't believe her, but what in the world can a person get their mother for Christmas that lives up to what they deserve? Pretty much nothing, especially when you're only twelve years old. Nonny got a little sick late in the afternoon and nearly threw up, but she drank some water and we relaxed on the couch and she said she felt better. I kept imagining all the things that could go wrong. There were so many ways Nonny or her baby could get sick. I tried not to worry *too* much, because it was Christmas, but that small worry cloud hovered there right outside my periphery nonetheless. (*Nonetheless* was a Hard Reading Word in English class last month.)

The worst thing was that Talia's grandmother died on Christmas Eve. When Talia texted me about it, I sat on my bed staring at my phone for five minutes. It didn't seem fair. I had to ask my mom about what to say back. I couldn't use a Silent Question with this one because I needed to say *something*. With Mom's help I wrote: *I'm really,*

really sorry. That's so sad. I'm thinking about you and I hope you and your family are okay and get to spend some good time together.

She texted back: *thanks.* She didn't text me for a few days. I didn't blame her.

There were so many big things happening: Nonny's baby, Talia's contest, Mr. Trent Hickman coming . . . every one of those things; plus, thinking about what Talia was going through seemed like its own Mount Everest. Putting those things together meant that on Christmas night when we were eating our billionth snickerdoodle and deciding which Christmas movie should be our grand finale and I settled onto the couch under my dad's arm, I never wanted to crawl back out again.

"Dad?" I said. "Is Talia going to be okay? I mean, I know not really, but . . . do you think there's still enough Good Pile stuff?"

Dad squeezed me tight. "That bad, hard thing is going to always be there," he said. "But absolutely the good things are always there, too. Talia's got at least one especially good thing that I'm aware of."

Did you know when your dad kisses the top of your head, you can feel the warmth all the way down to your toes?

The Impossible Dream

Somehow it seems strange when things go back
to exactly normal after a break. Back to Nonny
calling Thomas every night, because he was away
again, doing his dangerous job in the Florida Keys.
Back to lunches in the library. Back to homework.

Back to planning and editing.

Even Talia was home. I thought I could see the
sadness she was carrying in the gray around her
eyes, most of all when she tried to smile and wave
at me when I came to class. She didn't talk too
much, mostly stared at her pencil. And she worked
on her Poetry Out Loud contest harder than ever.
She passed me a note one day that said: *I'm really
sorry I can't do lunch again today. Gran told me*

to work as hard as I can and you better believe I'm going to.

When I got the note, I nodded to her. I didn't know a sign to say, *I'm still so sorry about your grandma but I know she's proud of you and you are going to do awesome in this contest and you do whatever work you need to do*, so I gave her a thumbs-up instead.

I got a note from someone new, too. Charise from the Lunch Table Girls passed me a note in the hallway that said she'd tried my mom's constellation cupcakes. Her note said they were *Out of this world delicious!* I wrote back *thank you* with five exclamation points and I knew the note would make my mom smile.

The Out of This World note made me more excited about math than I normally am. I knew people who wore NASA shirts had to be pretty great.

But I still missed Talia. I wanted to show her the note, but I didn't want to interrupt her focus. She needed to be ready to be a rock star at this poetry contest.

So I went back to going over my master plan, half terrified, half impatient for the day Mr. Hickman would finally show up. Only a couple of weeks to go. Apart from my essay, I had printed-out pages, cut-out pictures, glue sticks, tape, and a bunch of other crafty things spread across my room. I was going to be ready, that was for sure.

I talked the plan over with Cecilia almost every night.

Usually preparing and going over plans makes me feel better. That's why I like getting my homework done early, because it means I've planned and that when I walk in the doors the next day I know for sure I'm prepared.

I've tried to know for sure that I'm ready for the big things that are coming, but I'm still scared. Terrified.

Timorous. Another Hard Reading Word.

It means scared.

When Scared/Terrified/Timorous Me comes along she pushes her way in, shoving Regular Happy Me into a corner and sort of taking control of everything. If the two me's were at a party, Scared Me would be the one who started shouting and screaming and talking as loud as she could every time Regular Happy Me tried to talk.

So after school, I grabbed my stuff from my locker and decided to go talk to someone who never, ever seemed to be afraid.

She was sitting at her desk, looking at papers.

"Ms. Trepky?" I said.

She glanced up and when she saw me, she put her pen down and scooted the pages to the side.

"Ms. Monroe," she said. "What can I do for you?"

Then I didn't quite know what to say. I'm not usually scared to talk to people, but when the door has somehow been opened for Scared Me to move in, she kind of grabs the steering wheel and doesn't let go for a while.

"Well . . . ," I started. Maybe this really was a stupid idea. Maybe this wasn't something you talked to your teachers about, and I just didn't know. Probably everyone would think it was odd if they knew. Maybe even Ms. Trepky would think I was weird and awkward.

Ms. Trepky folded her hands on her lap. She had a smile that wasn't quite a smile because her mouth only moved a tiny bit, but it was more of an Inside Smile and I knew she wouldn't think I was embarrassing.

"Do you ever get scared? About doing something?" I said it all at once, fast, so I was sure to get it out.

Then Ms. Trepky looked down at her hands and smiled again, and it wasn't a You're So Cute smile, which would have made me want to cry, but a sort of Chuckling at Myself kind of smile.

"Let me tell you a secret," she said.

I stepped closer.

"Do you know what sound scares me more than any other?"

Scary sound? "Fire alarm?" I said.

"The school bell, first thing in the morning."

My eyes went big. It was like a tiger admitting she was scared of oinking. "The bell? Why?"

"Because it means it's time to get up in front of you and start teaching, and let me tell you a secret I think every teacher shares. Nothing is more frightening than teaching."

"But . . . but we're just kids."

"Exactly. You are our tomorrow, and we don't want to mess anything up."

"But if it's so scary how come you do it? How can you do it every day?"

Ms. Trepky scooted her chair back and leaned toward me. Even through her glasses I could see her looking at me very, very closely.

"How important are these things that scare you?"

I didn't even have to think about that one. "The *most* important."

She nodded. "Precisely. If they weren't, or if you didn't care deeply about them, they wouldn't scare you. And so you do them anyway."

"So how do you not be scared?"

"You don't," she said. "But you get better at the doing-it-anyway part, even when you risk failure. And that, in my mind, is the perfect definition of courage."

We were quiet for a minute, and I tried to make sense of it. Maybe there were also two Ms. Trepkys, the Regular Confident One and the Shy Frightened One. And maybe the Frightened Ms. Trepky made the same shrieks and screams and moans that Scared Me made. Maybe the trick for Confident Ms. Trepky wasn't knowing how to make the wailing go away, but learning how to dance to it.

"Thanks, Ms. Trepky," I said.

I didn't know if I was going to be able to be brave like Ms. Trepky, but I didn't really have a choice. I had too many important, scary things coming up.

"Libby," Ms. Trepky said. I looked back at her from the classroom door. She hesitated, mouth open like she was searching for words, and I waited. Finally she said, "Good work in my class, Libby."

A New Doctor

A few days after talking with Ms. Trepky my mom checked me out of school half an hour early.

I flopped into the backseat and dropped my backpack on the floor. It seemed like so many worry whirlpools—baby worry, Mr. Trent Hickman worry, Talia's worries—were swirling around in my mind into one big blustery mess.

"How was school?" Mom asked.

"It was good," I said, trying not to pick at my nails. Sometimes I did that when I was so focused and anxious about something.

Mom cleared her throat and looked back at me, so I knew she was going to tell me something important. "Honey, do you . . . do you remember when you were taking piano lessons and things were really, really hard? And I told you I'd look into something?"

I nodded. Was Mom going to sign me back up for piano?

Mom kept going. "Sweetie, I know things are going on with Talia and school and other things making you anxious and . . . well, if it's okay, I'm going to take you to a new doctor's office because I think they might have some ideas."

"A doctor? What kind?"

"It's called a . . . I think she's a neuroscientist. Or a psychologist."

"A neuropsychologist."

"Sure, that works. Is that okay? We're just going to talk to her."

My mom was looking at me, both hands on the wheel, and she looked nervous to be asking me this, like maybe it would hurt my feelings. I smiled at Mom and her shoulders relaxed.

"Okay," I said.

This doctor's office was in a brown brick building about twenty minutes away. This office had the puffy gray chairs, landscape paintings, and latex-and-disinfectant smell like my other doctors' offices. Mom checked us in, then a nurse in turquoise scrubs brought us to the back. Like normal.

Except this time it was slightly different. This time I didn't take my shoes off and stand on the scale, and this time they didn't take my blood pressure. And when we got to the office in the back there wasn't a doctor's table covered in paper for me to lie on. Instead, more chairs and a desk.

Then a woman came in who was only a few inches taller than me and had brown skin and the brightest smile. "I'm Dr. Prasad," she said, coming straight over to me. "And you're Libby?"

I shook her hand and smiled back. I already liked Dr. Prasad.

"Yes," I said.

And that's how the weirdest doctor visit I ever had began. Dr. Prasad asked me a lot of questions at first. She asked me if I liked school, and what parts I liked. I told her I definitely didn't like math. She asked me about my friends. She asked if it was hard for me to make friends. I told her I liked eating lunch in the library, because with doctors you're supposed to tell the truth, and I told her about Talia. She asked me lots of questions about how I had made friends with her. She asked me if I knew the difference between anxiety and fear and I said of course and she smiled and asked me if I felt anxious a lot.

Then we did some game-style tests. There were flash cards with symbols and sounds that I had to memorize, and a game on the computer where I had to click the space bar when I saw a certain letter. Some of the test games were easy and some were a lot harder than they seemed.

Then we waited a bit, and then Dr. Prasad and Mom went into another room and talked by themselves. I read a *National Geographic* magazine.

When they came back out I couldn't read the expression on Mom's face. It was almost like she'd been crying, but not. Like she was sad and also relieved, like she was gearing up and also ready to lie down.

"It was a pleasure to meet you, Libby," said Dr. Prasad. "Keep working hard in school."

I nodded.

"Thank you," said Mom, like she really meant it. Like after a couple of hours they were now the best of friends.

I was ready to leave, which was unusual for me and doctors' offices. Dr. Prasad was maybe the nicest doctor ever, but I felt like something that had been under the microscope for too long.

NLD

Mom and I walked out through the front office and took the elevator to the main floor without saying anything. I really wanted my mom to explain everything to me, but I was also trying to sort through everything that had happened and think it through in my head first, so being silent for a while was okay.

Then when we got in the car, Mom turned it on and turned the radio down.

"Remember when we told you about Turner syndrome?" Mom asked.

"Yes. We had chocolate cake. Are we going to get chocolate cake?"

Mom laughed. "If you want, but it's not quite

that kind of a chocolate cake moment. It's another part of . . . everything."

"The icing."

She looked at me. "Do you remember the boy in your third-grade class who took medicine for ADHD?"

"Do I have ADHD?"

"No, no, you don't, I'm trying to find an example . . ."

"Oh."

"And maybe that's not the right way to start . . . I don't know. I've never had to explain . . . But, well, everyone learns differently, right?"

I nodded.

"And there are lots of things our brains do."

"Yeah."

"Now," Mom said. "Your brain is working totally fine. It's just that a lot of times with Turner syndrome there's something else that happens that influences the way your brain learns things."

"Like ADHD does."

"Sort of, yes, but this is different. It's called a nonverbal learning disorder."

I looked at the deep line across the bridge of her nose. She still hadn't started driving. "I have a learning disorder?"

"I don't like that word," Mom said, and she kept talking, almost to herself. "The literature makes it sound . . . And she asked if you wanted special modifications or special testing . . ." Mom looked at me. "You don't need special help on tests, do you?"

"Special help?" I asked. "What do you mean? I ace my tests."

Mom looked ahead and nodded. "That's what I said." She took a deep breath, then looked at me. "But sweetie, this is part of why you . . . why you worry about things or get focused on things that are making you anxious. This is why certain things are especially tricky for you. Like learning piano."

I was so focused on trying to understand the worried way Mom kept looking at me that it took a second for the words to make sense.

"This is why piano was hard?" I said finally.

"Yes. A nonverbal learning disorder makes certain things more difficult, things that you can't explain in words. Or maybe when you're talking with people it's harder to understand the things they don't say out loud. Things like friends and piano stretch your brain in a really good way, but a hard way. Do you understand?"

Her eyes searched my face like a flashlight scanning words across a page.

I thought about Nonny's Silent Questions, and her long fingers hopping across the piano keys like jumping spiders. This was why it took me so long to figure out about Silent Questions. This was why I couldn't ever get my brain and hands to connect to the music no matter how much I practiced.

I didn't quite know how to feel about this new information, like it was both hot and cold at the same time. This was another way I was different. Another way I couldn't do things the way Mom and Nonny could. If they were graceful swans, was I always going to be a fuzzy little goose?

But on the other hand, this meant it wasn't my fault. This meant it was science.

I didn't need to feel bad about science. Right?

Or did this mean there were more and more things I couldn't do?

But then my mom said something.

"I'm really proud of you, sweetheart."

Proud? I didn't feel like anything to be proud of. I felt confused, trying to figure out how to fit the me that wanted to cry with relief next to the me that was stuck in a locked box with no key.

I looked at my mom.

She said, "You . . . I know you try so hard. With everything. That piano recital . . ."

"The one that went supernova bad?"

"No," Mom said. "No, it's like you played with your hands tied behind your back. And you got up and played anyway."

I looked at my knees. There was too much heat in the car. The hot-behind-your-eyes kind of heat, and what-if-there-are-lots-of-things-I-can't-do heat, and mom-is-proud heat. It's not that I would be embarrassed to cry when it's just my mom, but I never know what to do in that kind of heat. Such serious, somber heat. It makes me fidgety. I had to let out some of the steam.

So I sat on my hands, lifted my feet onto the dashboard, and started humming my old piano piece while wiggling my toes.

Mom laughed, and we pulled out of the parking lot. I hoped she knew what I was trying to say inside the joke. A different kind of inside joke.

And some of the behind-the-eyes-heat went away.

For now.

There's a Monster at the End of This Brain

That night Nonny looked pale. Paler than normal, which is saying a lot. Looking dangerously close to the gray-faced-nausea type of pale from before. She kept saying she was fine, but I could tell she wasn't feeling well.

I boiled some water and made her some orange marmalade toast and herbal tea. Mom and Dad were out on a date together, but Mom had taught me how to make tea, even though I'd broken a couple of mugs in the beginning. Still, though, it was kind of strange being alone in the kitchen.

Nonny was lying on the couch, her eyes closed, her long dark hair draping down to the floor, and if I was a good artist I would have wanted to paint her. I think it was the orangey smell of the tea that made her look over at me, and she smiled. I was glad to see a touch of color in her cheeks when she did.

"Oh, you. You didn't have to do that," she said.

I put the mug and the plate of toast on the coffee table by the couch. Nonny curled herself up and I sat down at her feet. She took the mug in both hands and breathed in the steam and sighed when she took a sip.

"Thank you," she said. "You're my favorite sister."

"I better be," I said.

She took another sip and a bite of toast. After a minute she said, "I heard you went to the doctor today."

I tucked my feet under me. "Yeah."

"Usually you like the doctor."

"Yeah."

"But not this one?"

"I liked her a lot."

Another sip of tea. This time I knew she was asking me a Silent Question.

"It's weird . . . ," I said. I didn't really know what exactly was bothering me. "It's hard to explain."

She kept going with the Silent Question.

"It's like . . . ," I started. "It's like they told me there's something sort of controlling how I think. I mean, not exactly, but something at least kind of influencing the way I think. That . . . that's weird. If . . . if that's true, if something in my brain really is different, then I . . . I don't know what's me and what's . . . controlling me."

"I get that," Nonny said. "But I don't think they mean something's inside your brain controlling you. It's the way your particular brain is built. It's you."

"But it's a different thing," I said. "I mean, it means my brain works a certain way. A different way. So then, what if I didn't have that thing? Wouldn't that mean I'm a different person?"

"Then you'd be a different person," Nonny said. "But you're not."

"I guess."

Nonny put the mug back on the table and sat up taller. "Think of it this way. Tell me something you learned at school today."

"Um . . . oh, we had an assembly about internet safety."

"So your brain is already different today than it was yesterday, right?"

"Yeah, I guess so."

"But you're still you, right?"

I couldn't help but smile. "Hey, no fair! Okay, you got me."

"There you go," Nonny said, and picked up her mug again.

I knew Nonny would understand. And I knew, without a doubt, that I would do whatever it took to give her this beautiful universe, this perfect baby. Sometimes, though, there were these what-ifs that shot across my mind like comets, flaring in and out. There were the normal what-ifs, like, *What if something went wrong?* But there were other what-ifs, too. Like, *What if I was the perfect, best, most understanding aunt in the world for a niece who had Turner syndrome, too?*

"Nonny?" I said.

She took a careful sip. "Hmm?"

"What if . . . what if the baby has a disorder?"

Nonny choked a little on her tea, but with someone as elegant as her, it was more a dainty cough.

"Have you been worrying about that?"

I pulled at loose threads in the hem of my shirt. Why was it so hard to think of the right thing to say at the times when saying the right thing was the most important? I could talk and talk for a long time about exciting things, but *explaining* what I really meant was different. "I mean . . . I wonder . . ."

Nonny put her mug on the table and put her

hand on my knee. I glimpsed one of those particular furrows between her brow and it made her
look like Mom.

I knew Nonny would love her baby more than
life itself no matter what, because that was Nonny.
And I knew that technically this baby wasn't any
more likely to have Turner syndrome just because
I had it. But things could still go wrong. Things
could still be hard. I didn't want something making things harder for baby Cecilia or Nonny. I
wanted things to be perfect.

"This baby is this baby," Nonny said. "Whoever
she is. And I'm her mother. That's all there is to it."

"And I'm her aunt," I said.

Nonny smiled and the Mom-furrow relaxed.
"Yes. Yes, you are." Then she made another sick
face for a split second, and I remembered.

"Oh wait," I said. "I'm supposed to be making
you feel better this time."

I ran to Nonny's bed and carried out her big quilt
that smelled like her—like her lavender shampoo—
and laid it across her lap.

"I have an idea," she said. "I was too tired to read
to Cecilia today, but how about you read to us?"

I bounced once on the couch. "Oh, I can read you
the book we're reading for school!"

"Which one's that?"

"*Charlotte's Web.*"

"Well, you are *some girl*," Nonny said.

So I ran to my room and got my book from my backpack and came back to my seat by Nonny.

When I finished reading the chapter Nonny's eyes were closed and her chest was rising and falling slowly. In sleep she looked less pained. Whatever it took, I would make sure she stayed that way. Her and baby Cecilia. Safe and happy and perfect. I stuck my feet under her quilt, laid my head on the other side of the couch, and closed my eyes, too.

Master Plan

Here is what else I did in the three days between my appointment with Dr. Prasad and the day Mr. Trent Hickman came to Boulder.

I had Ms. Trepky read over my Cecilia Payne Letter of Awesome one last time. I had the first two sections written and ready to go. Now I just needed to complete the project part and write that part of the letter. Then I'd be set for the grand prize.

I went over my master plan. Some things were easy, like what I wanted to say to Mr. Trent Hickman and studying the map of campus and the building where he would be. I was still scared, but I knew what to do. I had my supplies ready. Some other things weren't so easy. Campus was only about a fifteen- or twenty-minute bike ride away, which I could manage okay if I was careful and had a big coat, but Mr. Trent Hickman was coming on a Friday—a school day—and right smack dab in the middle of school. I didn't know how to work my way around that one.

I felt baby Cecilia kick four more times.

I helped my mom make a wedding cake for a client. By *helped* I mostly mean watched. Mom had all sorts of tricks for doing these fancy designs using only her right hand. It was like watching a painter.

I passed one note with Talia in class. I thought about what to say a lot before I wrote it down. I wrote: *How is your poem coming?* She wrote back: *Killing it. It's going to be bomb.* I gave her a thumbs-up, and she gave me a thumbs-up back.

Mom and I didn't talk much about NLD. I wasn't surprised. I kind of thought Mom didn't want to talk about it. Not because she was scared or uncomfortable or anything, but I think she was worried that if she told me too much, it would feel like reading my horoscope. Like she would be telling me all the things I couldn't do.

For the same reason, I didn't look up NLD on the internet, either. At least not yet. I wanted to talk to Mr. Trent Hickman first. In case the internet told me that talking to people like him was something I shouldn't be able to do.

Finally, the last thing to work out was my travel plan. I still wanted the contest and the money and everything to be a surprise, but I was going to have to tell my mom *something*. I thought through a thousand different options, but the only way to do it without Mom's help was lying or sneaking out, and there was no way that was going to happen.

So on the night before The Day, I asked my mom about it.

Mom was smoothing my moon-and-stars quilt across my legs like she did every night.

"Mom?" I said.

"Yeah?"

"I have to ask you something weird, okay? But I'm serious about it. And . . . and it's sort of a secret. Like, a surprise. Part of it is, anyway."

"Do I need to be worried about something?"

"No, no," I said. "Nothing like that. It's about that sort-of-secret project I've been working on in Ms. Trepky's class. Now I . . . I really, really, really, really need to ride my bike to the university tomorrow. Like, in the morning. I know it's a school day, but it's really important. And I don't have any tests tomorrow or anything and I already know what the homework will be for the weekend and—"

"Why do you need to go to the university? Getting your doctorate already?"

"I'm serious," I said.

"I know."

"I don't want to spoil the surprise too much, but this editor guy is coming to campus tomorrow and for the project it would be super, super awesome if I could talk to him."

Mom put her hand where my knees stuck up under the quilt. "Sweetheart, I get that this is important to you, but campus is a long way away by bike. And I don't like the idea of you walking around a college campus all by yourself."

"I already have it planned," I said. "I have a map, I'll have my phone, and I won't talk to anybody except to give this editor guy the thing I have for him, and—"

"Sweetheart, it's—"

"Mom, please. It's—it's the most important thing I've ever done. I have to do this."

Mom patted my knees and sighed. She kept patting and sighing and I didn't say anything because I didn't want to jinx it if she was thinking herself to a yes.

"Okay," Mom said finally. "How about this. You are already doing really well in school so I'm okay if you take the day off tomorrow. But *I* will drive you to campus. Hold on, just listen. I know it's a secret, but I will drive you to campus in the morning and then I'll walk you to whatever building you need to go to, and I'll stay nearby. And you have to call or text me every half hour. Is that a deal?"

I bounced up out of the quilt and wrapped my arms around her shoulders. "Deal!" I said.

It was going to happen. I was going to talk to Mr. Trent Hickman whether he liked it or not.

"Libby, I want you to understand that I'm letting you do this because you have earned my trust, okay?"

I wrapped my arms around her shoulders again so hard she made a sound like a deflating basketball and then laughed. "You're the best mom in the whole world!" I said.

This was actually happening. Like for real.

Like tomorrow.

Tomorrow.

I felt the Scared Me raring up for the biggest, wailingest scream of her life.

Like Ms. Trepky said, Scared Me could fuss as much as she liked. I was doing it anyway.

The Day

I woke up forty-five minutes before my alarm went off and couldn't go back to sleep. I lay in bed for a while, but soon enough I couldn't do that, either.

It was barely six thirty in the morning, but I got up and got dressed and packed my backpack. By then it was six forty-five.

The schedule was all worked out. Mom and I would leave at eight thirty. That meant I could get to the steps of the Norlin Library, where Mr. Trent Hickman was going to speak, by nine. His lecture wasn't scheduled until ten, and maybe an hour was overdoing it, but I planned to catch him on the steps of the library and talk to him about Cecilia before he even got inside. I thought that maybe if he was sort of rushed or had something else on

his mind, he would be more easy to convince—
that he'd listen to me, and take my letters that I'd
printed out nice and neat and carefully placed in
a manila envelope.

At seven I heard someone moving around in the
kitchen and smelled toast.

Mom and Nonny stood at the coffeemaker, watching the brown drizzle with tired eyes. Nonny's belly
was at full basketball status now, and had been
for a while. February 17 was coming fast, and even
getting up and down from the couch was hard for
her.

They both looked at me, and Mom laughed. "I
see you're dressed and ready to go. And barely an
hour and a half to spare!"

I was wearing my favorite purple sweater and my
yellow beanie. My black boots were by the front door.

It was one of the longest hour and a halfs of my
life.

Finally, Mom and I were getting in the car.
Nonny sat on the couch, glancing at us through
the front window. She was looking at a Pinterest
board of picture books. I watched her as we drove
away. She looked so . . . I couldn't think of the
right word. None of my best Hard Reading Words
seemed to fit what I was thinking. *Young* wasn't

quite right, and *weak* definitely wasn't. *Vulnerable* or *open*, maybe. *Eagerly defenseless.*

Eagerly defenseless.

Was that what she saw when she looked at me? Was that a good thing or a bad thing? Maybe that was why everyone around me wanted to help, wanted to make sure I wasn't hurt. What I did know for sure was that being a defender of the eagerly defenseless was the most important job I'd ever have.

Defend against a hurt family, a damaged or a split-apart family.

Right, Cecilia? I thought. *That's the deal.*

And then we were off.

UC Boulder is known for its pretty pine trees and mountains, but I couldn't pay much attention to that as we drove. Mom knew where I needed to go, and I spent most of the drive looking down at my backpack in my lap.

When we got to campus and Mom and I walked to the library, I watched my black boots step and step and step, and reminded myself over and over to ignore the Scared Screaming Me. Brave Me was in charge today.

Maybe because I hadn't been paying much attention to what was happening outside of my head, it kind of surprised me when we reached the library. I looked up and counted the square, peachy-colored columns across the front. I would stand by that one right there, at the top of the stairs.

Mom put a hand on my shoulder, and I blinked.

"Honey, see that coffee shop? I'll be right in there, okay?"

I nodded.

"Remember you need to text me every half hour."

I nodded.

"Are you going to be all right?"

I nodded.

"You sure?"

I blinked again. "Yes. I'm sure."

"Okay. I'll be right over there."

And that's how I ended up standing on the steps of the Norlin Library on the University of Colorado-Boulder campus, with a big poster of Cecilia Payne's face that I'd glued right in the middle and the words MR. TRENT HICKMAN, THIS IS CECILIA. I'd tried to carry it facing away from Mom while we walked, and she was nice enough not to ask questions about it. This surprise was going to make her happy, too.

I had also tried to draw a telescope in one corner, but I'm not super great at drawing so it didn't turn out very well, and I could have gotten my dad to help me with it but I wanted to surprise him, too, and everybody. Besides, it didn't matter too much, because I knew Trent Hickman could read the words.

Time felt like putty, stretching, then scrunching, then stretching again. People—college people— kept looking at me, but I barely noticed. And with strangers, I'm not so great at knowing what their facial expressions mean anyway, so I pretended they were all very nice. They probably were.

I started worrying about campus security. What if I was breaking a rule I didn't know about? What if someone reported me? What if a policeman came up and asked me what I was doing, or where my parents were?

And then someone did walk toward me.

Someone carrying a briefcase and wearing a brown suit, someone who had light hair the color of the peachy marble columns.

Someone whose picture I'd seen on the Knight-Rowell Publishing website a hundred times.

Here we go, Cecilia. Are you ready?

He was looking down at me, at my sign, one eyebrow raised. His lips opened to say something, but I spoke first.

"Mr. Trent Hickman?"

"Yes?" His voice was smooth and crisp, no gravel in it at all. "Are you—"

"I'm Libby Monroe. I've called your office a few times. I have to talk to you about something important."

"I need to—"

"This will be very fast," I said. "We use your textbook, *Survey of Modern America*, in my seventh-grade history class. It's a very good textbook, but I believe that there is something important missing. Some*one* important." The more I talked, the quieter Scared Me's screams became. I was ready. I knew what I needed to say. I was going to win.

"Look, I really need to—"

"Her name is Cecilia Payne. She was a professor at Harvard. She discovered what stars are made of. And more people need to know about her. More girls in school. So they can be astronomers, too."

"I have to get—"

"I'm writing a letter for a contest at the Smithsonian, about overlooked Women in STEM, and for part of it I need to do a project to teach people about Cecilia Payne, and I think the very best project would be to have her added into the text-book."

Mr. Hickman sighed. "That's great."

"Yes, it is. So will you please include her in the next edition? And then I can write about it for the Smithsonian contest. It's really important. She . . . she needs it."

Mr. Hickman looked back and forth between me and the front door. Then he shrugged. "Duly noted. I've got to get inside now, kid."

"So you'll do it? You'll put her in the book?" It was like my insides had become a flock of fluttering hummingbirds. I held out my envelope. "This . . . this is my letter. Well, two letters. One is my letter for the Smithsonian contest so far, so you . . . so you can read about Cecilia. And then a letter to you that explains everything. And it's got my email address in it so you can email me and let me know and . . . and everything."

He was already taking a step toward the door, but I held the envelope in front of him and he took it.

He took my letters.

"Yeah, okay," he said.

And he pushed through the glass door, stepping long and fast.

I watched him carry his briefcase and my letters into the front lobby.

And through the glass door, I watched him hurry to the lobby trash bin and throw my letters away.

The Night

I would write more letters.

I would call and call and call again until the high-pitched lady at the front desk knew my name just by the sound of my voice.

I would look up plane tickets to New York.

There had to be a way I could fly to New York.

Maybe there were other editors on the textbook.

Maybe they would listen.

I still had a bit of time.

More than two weeks until the contest deadline.

A few weeks until Nonny's due date and the arrival of baby Cecilia.

Listen to me, Cecilia Payne. She's coming. You've seen how hard I've tried. And I'll keep trying. I won't give up. But please, Cecilia, you can't give up on me, either.

Please.

I think Mom talked to me on the walk back to the car, but I barely noticed where I was stepping.

I kept telling myself to *Just think*, and I said those words to myself so much I *couldn't* think. I needed someone to tell me what to do. Someone to tell me how to fix this. I needed that hand that reaches down when the main character in the movie is about to fall off the cliff.

I'm falling off a cliff, I thought.

And then *that* got stuck in my head.

Falling falling falling.

When we walked in the door Nonny probably asked me what happened, but I didn't really hear her and I went to my room and booted up my computer.

I sat staring at my computer for a long time.

That's when something else happened that severed the day in two. Shattered it. If time was like putty before, this was when it broke in half, like that whole first part of the day fell into a river and floated downstream.

Because all of that was Before.

Because then things became After.

Because when the sun was setting, I heard something crash.

Because when I heard the crash, I ran out into the kitchen. And there was Nonny, broken pieces of a mug between her feet.

And water.

Water sopping her pants and puddling on the floor. Something smelled sticky sweet.

She was staring at the water, and then she looked at me, like a first grader about to fall off the highest curve on the playground swings.

Scared Me knew that expression very, very well.

I screamed for Mom.

For the second time that day we loaded into the car.

This time Nonny was with us. And Dad.

This time everybody knew where we were going.

Hospital

Nonny called Thomas on the way to the hospital. He said he would be on the very next flight no matter what. She kept having to stop talking and clench her fist. She looked frightened and in pain.

Would the baby have come now, weeks early, if I had convinced Mr. Hickman? If I hadn't failed?

Mom called the hospital on the drive in, so they were ready when we got there. They had a wheelchair ready for Nonny, and she and Mom went through swinging doors in the back. Dad and I waited in the waiting room.

Waiting room.

Suddenly, after the explosion of what had just happened, waiting was all we could do.

Waiting

I waited and thought about babies that come early.

I waited and thought about babies that are hurt.

I waited and thought about daddies who have to work far, far away trying to fix a financial black hole.

I waited and thought about mothers who are in pain.

I waited and thought about how this time it might be my fault.

I waited, thinking every minute about how my plan had failed and how delivering a baby takes a long, long time.

Big Doctor Words

I learned a new Big Doctor Word.

Cyanosis.

It means that the baby's nails and lips and skin are a bluish-gray color.

It means that there is not enough oxygen in the baby's blood.

Doctor Who Was Wrong

Maybe the Doctor was wrong.

Maybe the bad things *do* ruin the good things.

Maybe sometimes there are just too many bad things happening at once.

Maybe it's like your friend is swimming in grief and hard, hard work and you don't know where the life vests are. And the textbook people won't listen to you. And you figure out all the things you can't do.

And your sister has a baby too early.

And you didn't do anything to help.

Septal Defect

Here is the reason why the doctors took Nonny's baby away:

Think of your heart like a house. Two rooms on the bottom floor, two rooms on the top.

Nonny's baby has a hole in her house. A hole between the rooms on the top floor.

That is called an atrial septal defect.

And the doctors told us they had to open her up. Patch up the holey wall in her heart.

The next morning we were in Nonny's hospital room, waiting, frozen silent like the TV nobody had thought to turn on. Dad stood against the wall. We'd offered him a chair a long time ago but he'd refused. Couldn't sit down, he said. Mom sat by the window, looking at her hands. Thomas arrived about three minutes before they took the baby away. He was lying next to Nonny in the bed, one arm around her shoulder and one across her chest like he was a seat belt and Captain America's shield rolled into one. Nobody had moved in a while.

I thought that when we got home I would take down my posters of the muscular system and the Milky Way. Muscles got tears and holes. Stars hadn't heard my wishes. I'd tried to be a defender and my defenses had failed. I had failed. I couldn't do enough.

It had been one hour since they'd taken the baby away.

Ten minutes ago, a nurse told us they'd started surgery.

Sometimes you don't need an X-ray or stethoscope to see a hole in a wall. Sometimes it's right there in front of you, gaping. Sometimes you look at people in a room with you, and it's not only a hole in a wall, but a sunken roof, a shattered window, crumbling bricks, and a foundation with a crack right down the middle.

We will both have scars along our ribs, the

baby and me. We will both have patched-up hearts.

When I was thinking of things I wanted Nonny's baby and me to have in common, this was not what I had in mind.

Waiting Again

I only got to see baby Cecilia for a few seconds, behind a glass window.

Surgery on a tiny baby also takes a long, long time.

A Glass Box

Sometimes if you're a brand-new baby who had to have heart surgery, you stay in a glass box for a few days.

Sometimes if that brand-new baby is your new niece, and you have to go back to school anyway, there's a kind of glass box around you, too.

We weren't allowed to hold baby Cecilia. Even Nonny couldn't hold her yet. Every day that week when I came back to the hospital after school, Nonny's hand was stretched through one of the arm-size circles into the glass box where her baby lay, and she was stroking the baby's head and back. She never stopped stroking. Thomas stayed for as many days as he could, sitting with Nonny and their baby until he had to fly back to Florida.

The baby's glass box was called an incubator. It was actually made of a special kind of plastic, not really glass. (I looked up incubators on the internet.) It seemed terrible that she had to be boxed up inside it all the time, but actually it helped keep her extra safe while she was getting better from the heart surgery. It kept the germs away, and kept her nice and cozy warm, too.

But it still looked terrible.

I'm not sure what my glass box was made of. Whatever it was, it made the words my teachers said reach a few inches from my face and then bounce off again. It made everything in my head and everything I tried to say feel echoey and far away. It was like my private glass box had its own weather, its own ecosystem, and not a particularly sunny one.

I sat in Ms. Trepky's class trying to listen. One day she even played a song called "We Didn't Start the Fire" and then we went through each person and event mentioned in the song and she told us about them and normally that would have been the Best Class Ever but not that week.

Talia passed me a note in class. It said: *I heard what's going on. I'm really sorry.*

I nodded.

She started writing on another scrap of paper. It took her most of the class to write a few short lines. Five minutes before the bell rang she handed me one more note:

The sun is a star, we know
but there are too-bright days
days when someone you love leaves you for good
days when the tiniest bodies have the biggest hurt
when the sun shines full
and you want to ask
how dare you.

It wasn't until Talia handed me a crumpled paper towel from her backpack that I realized I was crying.

My Body Versus Me

Sometimes I wonder if I would be a different person if my body were different. Sometimes I'm not sure what is my body and what is really, truly *me*. I mean, when you're missing a chromosome, does that only change your body, or does it change who you really are? If I had a complete set of chromosomes, I know I would look a little different. Less odd, maybe. (No more FrankenChin.) I'd likely be able to have kids of my own one day. Would I still get obsessed about contests I'm not ready for? Probably. Would it be easier for me to talk to a friend whose grandma died, and would I be better at doing math homework in the hospital? Probably not.

I don't really know. I *don't* have all my chromosomes. All I have is me.

Home Is Where
the Heart Is

During class on a gray-blue day my mom texted me a picture.

Usually I was a good student, and kept my phone off and put away like I was supposed to. But somehow, the week after baby Cecilia's heart surgery, that didn't seem to really matter.

The picture mattered.

It was a picture of Nonny, and she was holding the baby.

For the first time.

When I got to the hospital after school that day, she was still holding her. She was sitting in a chair by the window, the tiny little body pressed up against her shoulder, head resting against her neck. Exactly like the picture. Like she hadn't moved.

I came into the room, and everyone was talking softly and moving slowly, like we were at church. I sat on the edge of the bed and looked at the baby.

It was stunning how different she looked outside of that glass box.

We sat there for a second, all of us looking down at that tiny person. She really was so tiny. Her fingers made tiny fists, and she kept scraping her nails along Nonny's shoulder, but Nonny didn't flinch. Normally baby Cecilia had little mittens over her hands so she wouldn't scratch herself inside that box, but at the moment she was wrapped in a blanket, pressed close against her mom.

Nonny looked at me, and said, "Would you like to hold her?"

For a second I couldn't answer. Should I hold her? I'd messed things up already. Who was to say I wouldn't mess them up again, and even worse?

Then I thought about what Ms. Trepky had said about courage. Nothing bad was going to happen. The whole room was full of adults who would make sure of that.

So I gulped, nodded, and sat down in the chair by the window.

And Nonny slowly, gently, settled baby Cecilia in my arms, like she was handing me the most important thing in the world. Which she was.

There was so much perfect in this tiny person I had to take it in bits at a time. She was awake and looking up at me. She had wide brown eyes like her dad, flecked with gold. And she had Nonny's delicate, perfectly arched lips. Those lips made a small pucker while she stared up into my face.

"This is your aunt," Nonny said, stroking the baby's thick, curly hair. "The best aunt in the world."

Very slowly, I unwrapped the blanket from around baby Cecilia's left side. There was the scar, wrapping under her arm. The skin was still swollen and pink. A tiny slash across the patched-up heart. The people who'd fixed her were heroes. They were scientists. They were magic.

I remembered right then about one of my favorite words. It's not a Hard Reading Word, but something I learned about on my own, in one of the documentaries I'd watched. It's a Japanese word: *kintsugi*. In ancient Japan, the expert craftsmen and artists didn't throw away their beautiful bowls and teapots when they got cracked. Instead, they melted down gold and filled in all the cracks, no matter how big. Filled in the cracks until the ceramic was traced and lined with shining gold, shimmering and even more beautiful than it had been before. The most beautiful thing they'd ever made. That's *kintsugi*.

And here was our new baby—filled and sealed and traced with the purest gold. I touched the scar.

I realized that Cecilia Payne had given me just what I'd asked for.

Baby Cecilia was here, breathing, alive in my arms.

That's what the scar meant.

And the scar made her perfect.

My People's People

That night, for the first time since baby Cecilia was born, I thought again about Mr. Trent Hickman.

In my brain he'd lost his privilege to a normal name. Now he was Mr. Jerkface McJerkypants.

I lay on my bed, my hands gripping my quilt, seeing him toss my letters into the trash over and over until my whole face started getting hot and I couldn't lie down anymore. So I paced back and forth in front of my posters. (I had put them back up when I got back from holding baby Cecilia.)

How could he do that? Who did Jerky McJerkypants think he was, ignoring me like that? Throwing away my letters? It was like the Worry Balloon that had taken up every inch of space in my brain and my heart was worn out, and had finally deflated after holding my beautiful, perfect niece, and now there was room for all this Mad to come storming in.

She was beautiful and perfect. *Did you hear that, Mr. Editor McJerkyJerk? She's perfect. She didn't need you.*

Then I thought about Cecilia Payne, PhD.

I stopped pacing and curled my toes in the carpet, trying to hold on to the thoughts swirling around inside. When I thought of Cecilia Payne I couldn't quite get a clear signal, like my Emotion GPS was telling me to go north and south both at once. I tried to hold still, tried to listen better to the signals, and for the first time, I tried to ask myself a Silent Question I didn't have words for.

I hadn't talked to Cecilia Payne in my head ever since the baby had arrived, because I was afraid of what would happen when I did. I was afraid I would be mad at her. I was afraid I would lose a hero. Yes, baby Cecilia was here and recovering and perfect, but was that because Cecilia had helped? Or had she ignored me, too?

But it was time to talk to her again.

Still, trying to figure out the words I wanted to say to her was hard, even by myself in my own room. So I turned the Silent Questions toward her.

After a silent minute, a clear signal finally came

through the static. It sounded like Cecilia, but also like Nonny and Mom and even a little bit like Ms. Trepky, all in one.

I knew she could make it, the signal said.

She has the same people helping her as you've always had.

She is strong, and when she can't be strong she has Nonny, and Thomas, and Mom, and Dad.

She will have friends, whether making friends is easy or hard.

She has scientists and angels and scientist angels looking out for her.

She has you.

First Period

The next day it finally felt like I was really back at school.

I had a million pictures of baby Cecilia that I wanted to show Talia. And when I thought of Talia, I remembered I hadn't ever asked her about how Poetry Out Loud went.

Before the first bell rang I ran to her locker as fast as I could, hoping she would forgive me for being a terrible friend. She was standing at her locker packing up books.

That's when I saw her face close up. Her eyes and mouth were crumpled like she was going to puke.

"Are you okay?" I asked.

"I'm fine," she said.

Her face looked a little ashy. She didn't look fine to me. "You sure? You feeling all right?"

"Yeah, yeah, just my stomach."

"Maybe you need to go home. Should we talk to the nurse?"

"No, no." She looked down at her shoes, now looking more embarrassed than sick. She twisted some of her curly, dark hair around her finger. She looked up and down the hall, then leaned in closer. "Actually, it's . . . I woke up and . . . well, I started my first period this morning. That's what."

"Oh."

She leaned back. "I'm really fine, it just feels weird right here." She patted a hand low, low on her stomach. "My mom was acting so weird, like I'd won some freaking trophy or something. She was like, 'Oh girl, my grown-up girl.'"

I didn't really know what to say, because I was worried that whatever I said would be the wrong thing. Besides, my brain kept saying mixed things to itself. I was glad that Talia had told me about it, because it's the sort of thing that you only tell your best friends. But also I knew I would never have a period like that. At least not on my own, not for a long time. I would need special pills when I was older to make me have a period. For hormone regulation and bone density reasons, according to the doctor, although Mom says that's still years away and she also said, "Man, it would have been nice to get you out of the whole stupid thing entirely."

So yeah, no normal getting my period for me, whatever that means.

But actually I didn't think about that for too long because I remembered that my mom was already proud of me, and then I started thinking about questions. Questions I'd never had to ask before. Like, did it hurt in a stomachache way or in a gut-punch way? How much blood was there? I'd heard that in a few years when I started taking the pills, I'd only have to get a period every three or four months and getting one *each* month seemed like it would be so draining and, well, a lot of blood. Did you have to wear a tampon right at the beginning? Did they make it hard to walk?

Probably not great questions to ask in the middle of the school hallway.

And there were other Big Girl things to talk about first.

"You sure you're okay?" I asked.

She nodded. "I . . . Sorry I haven't exactly been super fun lately. There's been a lot going on."

"Me too," I said. "And you don't need to be sorry for being sad about your grandma or working really hard on the contest. Totally okay."

"Thanks," she said.

"Sure thing," I said. "And thank you for . . . for being my favorite poet."

She laughed. "Well, no rehearsing during lunch anymore, so you want to eat in the library?"

I smiled. "Always," I said, slapping my hands together. "And speaking of, I'm really, really sorry I haven't even asked you about Poetry Out Loud yet. How'd it go?"

"Nah, no worries," she said. Then Talia smiled one of her rare, dimply smiles, and it was like we were right back where we left off. Maybe even better.

"Well?" I said, bouncing. "How'd you do?"

Talia grinned.

"I got second place."

I jumped and clapped some more. "That's amazing! You're amazing! Phenomenal!"

"I was sort of sad at first that I didn't win. Okay, more like totally pissed. But actually then I thought of you talking to that stupid dumb editor guy on your own and I was like, when I tell Libby about this, what will she say? And I swear I could hear your voice in my head being all like, 'Second place is just amazing and plus it means you'll be ready to kick butt next year,' and so that's what I decided to do. Hang my certificate on my wall and get ready for next year."

Have you ever had moments where everything is so exciting and wonderful and you have a friend saying that she's glad you're her friend and you're so *effervescent* (a Hard Reading Word that means vivacious and enthusiastic) that you can't use words, only make happy squealing noises?

"And what about the Smithsonian contest?" Talia said. "You still have five days before the deadline."

I put a finger on my locker. "But I didn't get Cecilia in the textbook."

"So? You still have five days to do a teaching project and finish your letter."

"Five days? That's not very much time. Plus, I don't know what my project would be. I can't do poems like you or play music or do painting or drawing or anything."

"Oh please," she said. "Libby, you're one of the smartest people I know. No way you can give up on twenty-five grand, girl. Even if you don't win, you have to try. You can totally think of something kick-butt to do."

"What is it with you and butts?"

Dustin Pierce was at his locker down the hall.

Hadn't he learned anything?

I started walking toward him.

"Hey," Talia said. "Don't, he's not worth it."

I kept walking.

"Hey, Dustin," I said.

He looked at me and huffed. He was quite a bit taller than me. "Oh no, it's FrankenChin."

"Who's your favorite basketball player?" I asked.

Dustin and Talia both stopped talking. Dustin's forehead crinkled in confusion. "Huh?"

"You like basketball, right?" I said. "That's your thing, isn't it? So who's your favorite player?"

"Well, Michael Jordan is the best of all time. Duh."

"Okay, so do you think Michael Jordan wasted his time putting butt pictures in people's lockers? Do you think he spent time thinking up mean names and things to call people or do you think he maybe focused on something more productive?"

"What are you talking about?"

"While you're sitting here being a butt-obsessed

butthead, some other kid is practicing free throws or learning plays or . . . something. I dunno. But if they're practicing and you're butt-picturing, who's gonna be better at basketball?"

Dustin slammed his locker and rolled his eyes. "Whatever."

When I walked back to Talia she was shaking her head at me, grinning. "You are so weird," she said.

"I know," I said.

"Back to the Smithsonian contest . . . ," she said.

I thought about the private, best-friends thing Talia had just told me and I finally thought of the right thing to say. Maybe practicing Silent Questions also helps you become better at figuring out what to say when you have to say out-loud things.

"Okay, Talia. I'm not giving up on the contest, but I need someone to help me with a new master plan. Would you maybe want to ask our moms if we could have a sleepover this weekend and I'll try and have a new idea for us to start working on? And I'll submit it on Tuesday. And also, there's something I want to show you . . . if you're not scared of needles."

She's Got the Whole World in Her Head

With new gel pens and an open notebook, I armed myself for some brainstorming so I'd be ready when Talia came over to help me put a new plan together. I walked around the house with the brainstorm cloud hovering over my head, my toes squooshing into the carpet like roots trying to pull ideas out of the ground. After months of working so hard on the old plan, it was hard not to get discouraged. So many people were counting on me. *I* was counting on me.

What could I possibly do in one weekend that would be worthy of winning? Worthy of Cecilia?

I wandered out into the living room where the baby slept in her mechanical swing, Mom, Dad, and Nonny nearby in the kitchen chatting about their days. Pacing back and forth kept the blood flowing, kept me feeling like I was trying *something*, even if the idea sparks seemed to slip away as soon as I saw them.

I tried lying down on the floor and staring up at the ceiling. I tried lying on the couch upside down. I did jumping jacks and played my stomach like a drum. The big idea door had closed, but there had to be a cracked window somewhere, right?

Where did plans and ideas come from, really, anyway? Maybe ideas were recipes the same way our bodies were. Recipes of the things we did and the people we knew and the stuff we learned. Every person's brain had ingredients other people's didn't. Nonny's brain had piano and babies and a special way of talking to friends on the phone. Mom's had the best pineapple upside-down cake in the world, and Ms. Trepky . . . well, Ms. Trepky's brain had a whole lot of stuff, which was probably why she was a teacher.

And Cecilia Payne's brain had held stars.

What about mine? What did I have to work with? I looked around the living room, this time as if everything from the side table to the smell of roast coming from the kitchen was a potential ingredient for a fantabulous new idea.

Baby Cecilia was awake. Wide awake, staring at me with her round brown eyes. Her hands clasped and unclasped, and she watched me like everything I was and everything I did was exciting and utterly brand new, which, to her, it was. What must it be like to have a brain like that, so open and filling with bright new bursts every second? A whole universe inside there, growing. This Cecilia had stars, too.

Cecilia's brain had stars.

Her brain had stars.

That was it. That was it! I froze in front of baby Cecilia, staring back at her, letting the idea settle in and take root before I moved too much and jostled it loose. Neither baby Cecilia nor I blinked while I watched the idea whirl around and form into something I could see.

The idea was audacious, oh yes. And it was going to work.

I bounced over to baby Cecilia and gave her a gigantic smooch on the top of her head.

When Talia came over, I would be ready.

Watch out, Smithsonian, I thought. *Libby has a brand-new plan.*

What Brains Are Made Of

When Talia came over the next day for a sleepover,
I told her my new idea.

She said it was audacious.

(And in case you were wondering, she is not
scared of needles.)

I didn't know if the Smithsonian people would
think this project was as grand as getting someone
in a textbook, but the idea was weird, and as fun
to make as Mom's cotton-candy pie. I had to at
least try.

The plan was going to take all weekend. It was
All Hands on Deck.

When you have a new audacious plan, you have
to take it step by step:

1. Mom called Principal Lopez to make sure this plan would be okay. She said it would.
2. Dad went to the store and bought three long black poster boards. Put together, they were twelve feet long.
3. Dad also went to the printer's and got nice copies of lots and lots of small, grape-size brain PET scans Talia and I had found on the internet. PET scans are a special type of picture that doctors take of someone's brain, and they glow a plethora of neon colors—blue, green, yellow, orange. When we were laying out the pictures and the posters and everything, Dad started getting excited, talking to me about layout and composition.
4. And when baby Cecilia was sleeping, Nonny helped us cut out all those brains.

It took the entire weekend, but by Monday, I had my project ready.

And it was quite the project.

Imagine this: You're walking down the hallway of your school, and you see a long, long black poster hanging on the wall by the front office. At first the poster looks like the night sky, with perfectly measured constellations. You see the Big Dipper and Orion's Belt and Capricorn.

When you step closer, you see that what you thought were bright neon stars aren't really stars at all.

They're brains.

Brains glowing in a black night sky.

Now that's something you won't forget.

And next to the brain-sky poster is another poster, a poster of a watchful, determined woman in black-and-white. You learn that her name was Cecilia Payne, and that she discovered what stars are made of. You learn about her job, about the people who helped her and the people who didn't. You learn that stars are made of a bunch of whizzing chemicals, and that thoughts are made of that, too. Plus something neon colored and maybe a little bit magic.

Magic like black holes and dreams and heartbeats.

Magic like teachers and chromosomes and friends.

You might look at the constellations and think, *What are MY stars made of?*

One Month Later

From: Sabaa Bukhari <sabaabukhari@smithsonian.org>
To: Libby Monroe <doctorlibby@bvsd.com>
Subject: Smithsonian Women in STEM Contest
Notification

Dear Libby Monroe,

I am delighted to inform you that you have been
selected as one of our divisional winners in the
Smithsonian Women in STEM contest. As a result, your
school will be the recipient of a five-thousand-dollar
grant for STEM education. This year, selecting our division
winners and the grand prize recipient was particularly
difficult due to the number of incredible entries we
received, and we are so pleased that you are among
our winners.

Your letter about Cecilia Payne exhibited knowledge, skill in research, craftsmanship, and passion. These are attributes we look for in our winners. We were so intrigued by your description of the brain-star sky display you put up at your school, and while we loved the photos, we wish we could have seen it in person. Your writing sparkles and inspires.

Again, congratulations! I am certain the world is going to see great things from you in the future.

Sabaa Bukhari,
Smithsonian Institution

When I Showed My Family the Email

My dad said: *"Albert Einstein, look out!"*

My mom said: *"I didn't know it was possible to be this proud of my kids."*

Nonny said: *"This is huge! You are remarkable, little sister."*

Thomas's message said: *Did you ever know that you're my heeeeero!*

Baby Cecilia said: *"Gaaa."*

My best friend, Talia, who was over for dinner said: *"Second place is amazing and plus it means you'll be ready to kick butt in the next contest."*

My brain said: *I DON'T KNOW WHAT'S HAPPENING.*

My brain said: *Is this a Good Pile thing or a Bad Pile thing?*

Was this Winning?

Or was this No Grand Prize for Nonny, Definitely NOT Winning?

On an Ordinary Sunday

Mom and Dad were visiting a friend who was in the hospital. At home it was just Nonny, me, and baby Cecilia.

Only a couple of days before Thomas's contract was up and he and Nonny and Cecilia would fly back to his parents' house in Chicago, and he would start looking for another job.

Lots of people had complimented my display at school. Ms. Trepky gave me extra credit, even though she said I didn't need it, and Ms. Lopez said she was very proud. I was proud, too. Winning in my division was wonderful, and I tried my best to only be grateful. But I still had that thought in my head wishing I could have done more for Nonny. Done everything that she deserved.

Had I proved anything to that Inside Mirror version of myself, or had I not?

I was out in the front room working on math homework (blech). I heard Cecilia cry. She had this low, bleating cry almost like a lamb, which somehow made it even more heartbreaking. When after a few minutes she hadn't stopped crying, I hurried down the hall to the bedroom.

Nonny never got mad when I woke her up from naps, so I wasn't worried about peeking my head through the door. Nonny wasn't asleep. She was pacing over by the window, bouncing Cecilia up and down in her arms. Cecilia's fists were clenched and her mouth was open in that wail that tugged your heart around like a dog on a leash. Nonny had baggy eyes and major bedhead.

"Everything okay?" I said. I knew it wasn't, but I didn't know what else to say.

Even Nonny's voice seemed stretched. "I just finished feeding her and I've burped her and everything. She doesn't want to stop crying, let alone sleep."

So I walked over with my arms out and before Nonny could protest too much, took the baby out of her arms, being careful to support Cecilia's little head like Mom had shown me. I'd had enough practice that even walking around with the baby in my arms didn't scare me anymore.

"I got it," I said. "You sleep."

"That's sweet, Lib, but . . ."

"No," I said. I tried to gesture at the bed with my head. "Sleep."

Nonny sat on the bed, but didn't lie down.

Cecilia gave a hiccup in my arms. "Nonny?" I said.

She looked at me, hand in her hair, Silent Question on her face.

"I'm sorry I didn't win," I said. "I tried really hard."

"Win?" she said.

"The Smithsonian contest. I mean, I won the division, but the grand prize was twenty-five thousand dollars, and that could have been for rent or a house or . . . Thomas could have come home."

Nonny stared at me. Her hair was messy, but her eyes were bright. I bounced baby Cecilia a couple of times.

"That's what you . . . ," Nonny said, then stopped.

"I'm sorry it wasn't enough," I said.

Nonny patted the bed next to her. "Come sit," she said.

I brought Cecilia over, still holding her high and bouncy, and sat next to Nonny on the bed.

"Libby," Nonny said. "I'm going to say something and I want you to listen, okay?"

I nodded. I thought of another Hard Reading Word: *apprehensive*.

"There's really only one thing I want for my daughter. The ways Thomas and I figure out how to take care of our family—and we will—don't matter. I know I've . . . I've been anxious and stressed about money and job stuff, but we're going to figure it out. But you know what *does* matter? What I want more than anything for my daughter to have in her life?"

Nonny put her hand on the bed so her arm was around me, and took Cecilia's fingers in her other hand.

"I want," she said, "for my daughter to have someone brave to look up to. Braver than I could ever be. Someone so selfless they don't even realize it. Money has nothing to do with what I care about, as long as my daughter grows up to be like you."

That's when something inside me multiplied, expansive and warm, a quiet supernova. I held Cecilia tight to me, and leaned in to Nonny. The three of us sat that way for a long moment in Silent Closeness.

I'd been wrong before. Defending the eagerly defenseless didn't mean that nobody got hurt, or that you didn't get hurt. Because hurt was just there, part of the grass and the trees and the clouds and the burning stars. What defending meant was taking in the wounded when the hurt did happen, never budging, never wavering no matter what. Being a constant, bright North Star in a twisting, swirling sky. The scars and bruises given or taken were just part of the star chart.

And nobody was luckier—nobody had brighter, warmer, more glowing North Stars of their very own—than me.

"I'm going to miss you," I said.

"Desperately ditto," Nonny said. "We'll video chat all the time."

Cecilia's wails started again and I bounced her up and down. I put a soft kiss on the top of her head. "Can I . . . can I help right now?"

Nonny's shoulders slumped, tired. "Yes, please," she said. "Thank you, thank you."

"Okay, one second."

I laid baby Cecilia on the bed and as her wails

ramped up, dashed out to the front room and grabbed a book. When I came back, Nonny was lying next to the baby, stroking her head like she was trying to smooth Cecilia with calm.

I lay down next to them and blew raspberries on Cecilia's belly, which distracted her enough that her wailing volumed down to occasional *meep*s. Then I held the book over Cecilia's face. She liked the bright cover.

I opened to the first page.

"'This little piggy went to market,'" I read.

I took Cecilia's tiny fingers in mine. "Hmm," I said, "yours actually aren't very piglike yet, are they? Especially for a baby. Your piggies are still small. They're actually called phalanges. And the part right here below your knuckles are your metacarpals."

When I looked at her face, she was staring at me. Those big, brown, gold-flecked eyes were wide. The doctors had said she was doing well, but it was those gold flecks that really told me she was going to be okay. Girls with gold in their eyes were here to do important things.

She wrapped her hand around my finger. I read a few more pages of our book. Then baby Cecilia yawned, and then I yawned. Nonny's eyes were already closed, and she was breathing deep. When I finished the book baby Cecilia's eyes were closed, too. I watched her stomach rise slowly, and fall. Rise and fall. I laid my head next to hers and closed my eyes.

What You Do with History

Even though it wasn't my birthday or anything, on the day of my Cecilia Payne presentation, Mom made me chocolate Malt-O-Meal for breakfast. Dad put a doodle in my lunch bag, a sketch of me and Cecilia Payne swinging from the two long arms of a star.

I knew my PowerPoint rocked. I had worked and worked on it until it was worthy of its subject. I was ready.

"She was born in 1900 on May tenth," I told my class. I showed them pictures of Cecilia with her flapper curls and dresses. She was smart *and* stylish. Dustin didn't even have anything to make fun of.

"She studied astronomy. She was the first female department chair at Harvard. She figured out that stars are made up mostly of hydrogen. So essentially, yes, Pumbaa in *The Lion King* was right, stars are big balls of gas."

I heard giggles, which made me happy.

I told them about how Cecilia studied the structure of the Milky Way. I told them about how she was the first person to earn a doctorate degree from Radcliffe College.

"A while ago I actually tried to get her into our textbook," I said. "I know that wasn't part of the assignment, but I mean, she discovered so much about stars so I thought she should be in it. It didn't go so well, though."

Then Dustin *did* raise his hand.

Even though I was scared he would make fun of me, I called on him.

"Why don't *you* write a book about her?" he asked.

Ms. Trepky's grin reached clear up to her dark hair and I'd never seen her look so proud. "That," she said, looking between Dustin and me, "is an excellent idea."

I finished my presentation, and I was glad that I'd practiced it a lot and worked hard on my slides because part of my brain kept thinking about Dustin's idea. I knew I'd need a lot more time to think about it. Could twelve-year-olds write books?

Later in class, Talia recited a poem she'd written about Ala Tamasese, one of the leaders of the Women's Mau: Female Peace Warriors in the movement for Samoan independence. Talia wore a navy-blue lavalava with a white stripe and said that's what the Female Peace Warriors of Western Samoa wore. Nobody else did anything quite as memorable as that. Then Dustin showed a video he made about James Naismith, who invented basketball, and even though a lot of the video was mostly Dustin showing off his free throws, he still told us about how early players used peach baskets as hoops.

Every student worked hard on their presentation. Even Dustin tried his best on his movie, and it made me think that he liked this class, even if he'd never admit it. Ms. Trepky must have secret powers to put that spark in someone like Dustin.

I imagined having lunch with Talia and Ms. Trepky for years and years, until Talia and I were grown-ups. I wondered if it was weird imagining having lunch with your teacher, but I didn't care. I didn't care, because I knew how good a person she was to talk to, just like Cecilia and Rosalind and Eleanor Roosevelt. Thinking about having lunch with Ms. Trepky and Talia forever and ever made my insides start to swell like I was going to need heart surgery again. Everything in the classroom, every little pencil and every scuff mark on the floor, poured meaning and happiness into me until it was almost too much for a body to hold. And that was only the stuff *inside* the classroom. There were also the stars. There were my parents and my sister. There was Cecilia and baby Cecilia. Especially there was baby Cecilia.

Looking around at all that world, I think being born with a heart three sizes too big is worth the scars.

Seventh/Eighth-Grade Division Winner of the Smithsonian Women in STEM Contest

Dear Judges,

Listen. I may be a young girl, but I'm writing to you about something important.

My teacher once said that if we had a textbook that included everyone that mattered, we'd need a textbook of everyone. I think that's true. But today I'd like to tell you about one special person missing from my textbook.

Cecilia Payne was an astronomer who discovered what stars are made of. She wrote about it in 1925, in her PhD thesis at Harvard University. Someone else told her she was wrong but then published similar results several years later. But now Harvard University, where Cecilia was a professor, has a lecture series named after her.

Cecilia was born in England, but in her time, the only job she thought women could have in her country was teaching, so she came to the United States for more options. As she studied astronomy, she figured out that the sun and the other stars were made up mostly of hydrogen, even though at the time most people thought something very different. She also studied the Milky Way, and the evolution of stars.

Because of everything she found out, she didn't just change the world; she changed how we thought about the whole universe.

I have a genetic disorder called Turner syndrome. This means I have only one X chromosome, instead of two like other girls. This is one of the things *I* am made of. I am also made of marmalade toast and a love of lab coats. I am made of my family, including a brand-new niece who is also named Cecilia. We both have long scars from where we had heart surgeries. Stars are made of whizzing, flashing chemicals and power and heat, and maybe scars are what show us that we're made of all that, too.

This is one of the ways Cecilia Payne is an inspiration to me, as a girl with Turner syndrome. She figured out new and marvelous things about stars and the galaxy even though lots of people thought she couldn't. She figured out that even though some stars are big, some are small, some are red, and some are white, some are round or lopsided or spotted, they're all made up of the same stuff.

Maybe Cecilia felt a little bit different as a woman in the Astronomy Department at Harvard in the 1920s. I know sometimes I feel different as a girl with a missing chromosome. But when it comes down to it, when you get down to atoms and the humanness that holds our atoms together, we're all basically made up of the same stuff, too.

That's why, for my educational project on Cecilia Payne, I decided to make an exhibit at my school that combined stars with beautiful scans of the human brain. For my project I created a long black display of the night sky, with precisely measured constellations, but instead of stars I used small cutouts of colorful PET brain scans. They glowed pink and green and blue, perfect against the black background.

When students at my school walked past this exhibit, they also saw a poster of Cecilia Payne, complete with her story about discovering what stars are made of. They read about her, learned her name, and might now think about her whenever they look up at the night sky. Or, maybe, when they wonder what *they* are made of.

This wasn't always my plan for my educational project. I had another idea, an idea that I worked at for a long, long time. But like Cecilia, I ended up having a hard time getting people to take my idea seriously. The people I needed for that project weren't quite ready to listen. At first I wanted to give up, to put my "PhD thesis" in a drawer, but if there's one thing I learned from Cecilia, it's to keep looking up, to figure out what you're made of, and to keep working at your ideas, not wasting time or energy blaming other people. A new idea sparked, and this time I had the right people around me, and we were ready to go.

Does knowing these things about stars really matter in one person's life? I say absolutely. It's the perfect reminder that anything that seems too big or too bright to understand, or too far away to reach, is really just made up of ingredients you've been working with your whole life. Ingredients that make up *you*. When there's the thing you know you're meant to be, whether it's a baker or a teacher or a neuropsychologist or a mother or a football player or a NASA technician or a rap artist, everything you need is already there.

I think if Cecilia were here today, she would say, *I discovered what stars are made of. Are you ready to find out?*

Libby Monroe
Camilla Junior High

Acknowledgments

First thanks go to my parents. Only one of you messed up when giving me my DNA, but I owe you both thanks anyway. Thank you for always believing in me and treating me as if I was just as capable as anyone else; for never once considering a missing chromosome as something that should, would, or could hold me back; for always having stacks of books all around the house and for not batting an eye when I told you I wanted to be a writer.

To my siblings, I blame all seven of you for making everything I write a "sibling story." Thank you for being excited with me. I raise this Disneyland churro in your honor. And to my grandparents, my roots, my safety, and my forever support.

To Dr. Swineyard, the greatest pediatric

endocrinologist in the world. The bit about liking doctors' offices is your fault.

This book is only possible because of the small army of incredible writing teachers I have behind me. This army stretches back to my first middle school and high school English and creative writing teachers, Mr. Matt and Mr. K. There's maybe no greater gift you could have given than genuine belief and interest in the first writings of a thirteen-year-old, so thank you. Thank you to John Bennion, Chris Crowe, Dawan Coombs, Bruce Young, Steve Tuttle, and all the incredible English department faculty at Brigham Young University. A special thank-you to Martine Leavitt, in whose class I wrote the first draft of this novel. That my return for an MFA and your semester as visiting professor happened to coincide was not, I will never believe, coincidence.

A huge thank-you to all the incredible writing friends and supporters I've made over the years. To Kim, Jessica, Jen, Tiffany, Bridey, and Roommate—my miracle friends. To Kristy, Tesia, Amanda, and Madeleine—for letting me be weird even in graduate school. To Elise-Merry, Amanda-Pippin, Kinner-Sam and Bobbi-Frodo—from Sarah-Smeagol, for letting me be weird from the very beginning. To my North Star mentors, Cindy Baldwin, Amanda

Rawson Hill, and Ellie Terry, all the other amazing Pitchwars mentors, and to my incredibly supportive Pitchwars '16 crew. I would truly be lost without you.

To Brianne Johnson, superagent and fairy godmother. Thank you, thank you, for being the first to see Libby's story and believe it deserved to be told. You are a magic maker and wish granter, and I can't believe how lucky I am that I was found by someone as masterful as you. To Brianne, Allie Levick, and the rest of the Writer's House crew, thank you. And to Melissa Warten, for championing this book and for edit letters that inevitably make me whistle and go *dang she's good*. If this book shines it's because of you. To Melissa and the whole team at FSG/Macmillan, thank you for taking me and Libby on.

Lastly, to all the girls born with a missing chromosome. I know each of us has a different story with Turner syndrome, but I wrote this for you. I hope more than anything to meet you one day, and if you want, you can use the code word *Cecilia Payne* and I'll give you a giant hug. You are what stars are made of. Here's what I believe: I believe the maker of stars, the maker of the whole universe, made you. And *you* are his most perfect and precious creation, just the way you are.